Shadows of Lost Time

Also by Kanwarpreet Grewal

The Parched Well: Poems

Shadows of Lost Time

Stories

Kanwarpreet Grewal

Copyright © 2011, Kanwarpreet Grewal
ISBN-13: 978-1460948835
ISBN-10: 1460948831

All Rights Reserved. No part of this book may be reproduced or transmitted in any form or by any means, electronic or mechanical, including photocopying, recording or by any information storage and retrieval system, without the written permission of the author.

Cover photo © iStockphoto.com/webking

To my parents who have given me a beautiful life and infinite possibilities

Contents

To The Reader 11

The Past 13

Dear Anju, Dear Olga 15
Was Xanthippe a Shrew? 36
A Story Hidden in the Depths 59
The Conquest 82
No More a Roving 110
Renaissance 131

The Present 157

The Double Helix 159
Sunrise 174

The Future 191

The Wall 193
The Message 202

And then he drew a dial from his poke,
And, looking on it with lack-lustre eye,
Says very wisely, 'It is ten o'clock:
Thus we may see,' quoth he, 'how the world wags:
'Tis but an hour ago since it was nine,
And after one hour more 'twill be eleven;
And so, from hour to hour, we ripe and ripe,
And then, from hour to hour, we rot and rot;
And thereby hangs a tale.'

From *As You Like It* by WILLIAM SHAKESPEARE

To The Reader

Dear Reader,

Time is the thread that connects the past, present and future of our lives in a mysterious unending chain. The flow of time surrounds us and we swim in its current, yet what we know as the present is an infinitesimal fragment of what is past and what is yet to come. We experience time in transitory moments and then it is gone forever. But time that is lost in the past, time being lost in the present and time that will be lost in the future casts its shadows on our minds: faint, diffuse and fleeting shadows of what has been, what is, and what will be.

In this book I have tried to form images of these shadows of time that arose in my mind in the form of stories.

This book is divided into three sections. The Past is the first section and the stories are about real historical events or people. Certain aspects have been fictionalised to present a different way of looking at history. While writing, I often wondered if I had the right to weave fact and fiction into the fabric of the same story but my mind was put at ease when I remembered that historical 'facts' are themselves a complex mixture of truth, imagination and myth. We do not really know the past: we merely see shadows of lost time and each one of us has the right to interpret what these shadows may mean and to try to illuminate the real events that cast them.

Shadows of Lost Time

The two stories in the second section are set in the present in the modern city of Delhi. In both these stories, the passage of time radically alters the fate of the characters. Time takes away what was precious but then offers something of immense value. Choice. The choice to interpret what has been given and what has been taken away by time; the choice to discover oneself by understanding the shadows cast by time past; and the choice to change the future in the flow of time.

The third section is about the shadows cast by the future on the present. These stories can be termed science fiction, but classifications are limiting. They were born out of a desire to find explanations for unsolved mysteries in our present through stories set in the future. However, when the future becomes the present, my imagination will, I am sure, pale before the astonishing reality that will unfold.

A brief explanatory note is included at the end of some stories so that the reader is aware of what are accepted or known 'facts' and which parts of the story are my imagination.

I would like to thank my editor, Deborah Smith, for her excellent feedback, eye for detail and immense patience that has helped me to express these shadows in the form of this book.

Kanwarpreet Grewal
New Delhi
1st September 2011

The Past

This is the place.
Stand still, my steed,
Let me review the scene,
And summon from the shadowy Past
The forms that once have been.

From "A Gleam of Sunshine" by H.W. LONGFELLOW

Dear Anju, Dear Olga

14th November, 1987

Dear Anju,

    I hope you are having a good time at Granddad's house. I know you will be back home before this letter reaches you, but I will still write. I am so excited to tell you something. Today, Mama and Papa took me to the children's fair at the Rose Garden. The entire garden was full of stalls selling books, toys and games. Papa told me that I could choose anything I wanted for up to 20 rupees. I bought a book titled *Physics Can Be Fun*. It looks like a very interesting book.
    After that, we all ate *samosas* and drank cola. It really was a very enjoyable day.

Your brother,
Kanwar

Shadows of Lost Time

21st May, 1941

Dear Olga,

My dear little sister! How long it has been since I last saw you. How is little Sasha? And how is Gregory? Write about them. Write about yourself. Write about what you do all day.

Today was an unusually sunny day here. It was so wonderfully warm and beautiful. And yes, last night was one of those white nights that our beloved city is so famous for. Whenever I venture out on one of these nights, I am reminded of Dostoevsky's words from his story "White Nights": *It was a wonderful night, the sort of night that can only occur when we are young.* Anna and I took a long walk in the Letiny Sad. The flowers were in full bloom and the fountains were lovely. We wished that you were here, along with Sasha and Gregory.

The madness may soon begin. But do not fear, my sister; the Madman shall quickly be overcome.

With my love,
Yakov

Dear Anju, Dear Olga

17th November, 1987

Dear Anju,

Physics Can Be Fun is, indeed, a fun book. I love reading it. And physics *is* fun. I am getting an amazing new perspective from every page. I have even done a few experiments from the book. Do you know why a drawing looks left-right inverted when you see it in the mirror? Do you know that railway tracks expand in summer? Do you know how a man can become invisible? Do you know what will happen if we dig a tunnel right through the centre of the earth?

It is a beautiful world of facts and knowledge. Come back. I have so much to tell you. I have found my path!

Today Mama made a delicious rice pudding. I ate it and you did not get any of it. Ha, Ha, Ha.

Kanwar

20th June, 1941

Dear Olga,

I hope that you all are safe and healthy. It is a difficult time for us all. The Madman is making everyone around him mad too, and they have set out to trample upon the flowers of hope that we so lovingly planted in our minds.

Today, we were told that we must help to protect each other. And we all vowed that we will. I have been digging all day and there are others who dig at night. I found a little rest after dinner and I wanted to speak to my little sister.

Do you remember how happy we were in school? Do you remember how I used to chase you in the garden and how we used to talk for hours and laugh without reason? And do you remember the cakes that we used to steal from Aunt Maria's house. They were so delicious.

If we were still children would it have been better?

How I wish to see you, Olga. Will I see you soon or will it be next year? No! I must not say next year; it has to be this year. I will see you before the autumn.

I *will* see you soon. As soon as this madness ends... very soon.

May mother bless you all,
Yakov

6th September, 1990

Dear Anju,

People in my class find physics and mathematics difficult. They are stupid. Physics is the most interesting subject in the world. Today, I showed the whole class an experiment that demonstrated surface tension. I filled a glass to the brim with water and then I dropped a pin – slowly - into the water. And then another. And then another. In the end, I must have added about 50 pins to the glass that was already full to the brim. The water bulged over the edge of glass, but it did not spill. The water seemed to be held there by an invisible force that defied the force of gravity. The class was astonished.

Physics is the study of nature. And nature is beautiful. Any brain that cannot understand this fact is a brain that has no understanding of what beauty means. Silly people!

E=mc2,
Kanwar

26th July, 1941

Dear Olga,

There is cheer all around. It is so difficult to face uncertainty when alone, but when friends are together, it is easy. I have more than a million friends today. Thousands of us walk every day to dig. I dig near the Luga. We will dig until we reach the Chudovo. We sing songs while we work. It feels good to do things together. We are brimming with hope. We are together in this and as long as we are together, we will never lack hope or happiness. We share our food and it becomes even more delicious. Now, I understand what it means to share. Now, I understand what our beloved leaders have always told us about the power of coming together, working together, and sharing whatever we have.

But, sometimes, when I turn on the radio at night and I hear of the terrible events that are happening, I feel fear and despair. The Madman talks and talks. I hope no one listens to him. Why can't people listen to Mozart instead?

So, I change the channel or play Tchaikovsky on my gramophone. Such happy music. Such cheer. Such glorious strains.

Anna has no worries at all. She still believes in God. She believes that all this is happening for the good. I hope she is right. At times like these, it is better to be innocent than to have knowledge.

Yours,
Yakov

4th May, 1992

Dear Anju,

I hope you're having a good time on your camping trip to Manali with your Girl Guide friends. I find your

Dear Anju, Dear Olga

Girl Guide salute so funny and your uniform...well...so quaint.

I know that you will be home before this letter reaches you but I will still write. I am full of frustration so I have to share my feelings with you.

Mama and Papa do not understand my love for physics. They say that there is no money in physics. I do not care about money. I care about the greatness of thoughts. They want me to apply to an engineering college. They say that physics is part of engineering. But that is applied physics. I want to study pure physics. I want to become a scientist and think about the universe. Who cares about computers or building materials?

I find solace in the library. *The Feynman Lectures on Physics* are almost a religious experience; a way to connect to the highest that the human mind can fathom.

And I read some inspiring lines which, for me, capture the exalted spirit of science:

> To see this world in a grain of sand,
> And the heavens in a wild flower,
> Hold infinity in the palm of your hand,
> And eternity in an hour.

Love,
Kanwar

Shadows of Lost Time

8th September, 1941

Dear Olga,

It has been several months since I heard from you. I pray that you all are in good cheer and good health.

They have come. It was a terrible day for us. There were so many frightening and terrible rumours going around. Some said that the Madman is with them; others that they are already within the city walls; or that they have surrounded us near Lake Ladoga. No one knows what is really happening.

We heard awful sounds around us all day: the thunderous crash of roofs falling in and buildings collapsing; children screaming. Fires broke out everywhere. I am terrified by all this noise. The roads are dark and dirty and the eyes of everyone you see are full of fear. I am exhausted, unable to find even a minute to rest.

When I returned home in the evening, something magical happened. I saw the most beautiful sight in the world. Anna was at the stove cooking broth that was so delicious that the warmth of its aroma filled the house. The light of a candle fell on her peaceful face as she stirred the soup, and it glowed like the face of an angel. She smiled gently as she sang an old peasant song. As I entered, she looked at me and put her arms around me and said, "Nothing will happen to us." Tears flowed down my cheeks because her embrace reminded me of Mama when she hugged me after I had broken Papa's chair. She had said the same thing, "Nothing will happen,

Yakov." Nothing had happened then. How can anything happen now? My worries, my fears, were all gone. In that moment, I followed her silly hope that only good would happen to us. I knew that she was right. She has to be right. All our life, Anna has followed me and I have told her what to do. Today, I followed her. I wanted to hold her hand and learn how to walk in this mad world. I wanted to cry on her shoulder and sleep peacefully with my head on her lap.

I know that this letter will not reach you now, so I will not even post it. I will just collect all my letters and give them to you when we meet. And I will scold you for not writing to your brother. You will be made to feel very guilty. I love you, my silly little Olga.

Yakov

18th August, 1996

Dear Anju,

How is college going? I hope you are not afraid of dissections. They are an important part of your medical education. How is the food at the hostel? Have you made any new friends yet?

I have a little notebook and I have named it *Questions in my mind*. In this notebook, I will write down all the questions that I still do not have an answer for. One day, these will be my research topics. I will never tie myself to one field of interest. I will never be the 'specialist' who knows more and more about less and less. The entire landscape of knowledge will be my field. I will roam in that landscape armed with the sword of my mind and with a heart filled with a burning desire to know. And I will gallop on a magnificent horse - the horse of scientific method. Life is to know. Life is to learn. Life is to honour the most precious possession that one has - the mind.

> Go wondrous creature! Mount where science guides
> Go measure air, weigh earth, state the tides,
> Instruct the planets in what orbs to run
> Correct old time, regulate the sun!

Kanwar

12th December, 1941

Dear Olga,

    Food and fuel supplies have been cut off and food is now severely rationed. Each day, we have to walk about 2 kilometres to get our ration of 125 grams of bread each.

Sometimes the bread is so damp and full of mould that I feel like throwing it back in the face of the person who distributes it to us. It is terrible.

Anna finds it difficult to walk all the way to get her ration. But they will not give her share of bread to me. Last week, I went alone and took both our ration cards with me to the relief camp. They would not give her bread to me. They said she had to come herself to get her share. I was heartbroken. I took my share of bread and gave it all to her and told her that I had eaten mine on the way. That was a terrible day followed by a sickening night. I felt so much pain and weakness from hunger. I felt such anger at what human beings think of as bravery!

Millions of years of evolution should have lead us far beyond the basic instincts of animals. Our progress as a species over the last few thousand years has been in the realm of the intellect; we create music, art, philosophy, science that is far removed from the basic needs of survival. But in war, the animal within us dominates and we destroy, we kill, we seek to inflict physical pain: to pierce the heads and hearts of our enemies. Why can't we fight each other's intellects? Why don't we attempt to puncture the ideas and thoughts of others instead of harming them physically? We are forced to bear the terrible consequences of the greedy and egotistical quest for land with our hunger and deprivation. This is not bravery!

There is nothing honourable in war. When you admire the painting of a battle scene with the triumphant winner raising his sword with pride, look carefully at the carnage that surrounds him; the dead and dying men, and the burning homes of simple village folk, their women raped and killed, their children orphaned. Is this the glory of battle? Is this courage?

They say it is brave to fight. Is it brave to march in rows behind one man to a silly repetitious tune, all dressed alike and determined to kill or die? Is it brave to thrust your bayonet into the chest of a screaming man and then to receive a medal for it? Napoleon was not brave! Alexander was not brave! They were mad, and their followers were brainless asses.

Is it not courageous to uphold and stand up for ideas? To follow an idea or instinct for years knowing that the chances of success are minimal; to challenge two thousand years of ridiculous superstition even though you are considered a lunatic or heretic. Galileo was brave. Copernicus was brave.

It is very cold and dark here. The trees in the parks and gardens have been cut to use as firewood. The landscape is barren and dejected and smoke casts a grey pall over it.

I can hardly believe what I have heard: that people are killing and eating each other and the police have formed a special unit to counter cannibalism. There have been horrific stories of starving people eating rats, their own pets and even the sick and dying. Does such disgusting behaviour arise from bravery and courage?

Dear Anju, Dear Olga

What has happened to our world? What will happen to us?

Yakov

15th August, 1998

Dear Anju,

The last few months have been very happy for me. Life looks so brilliant and colourful when you see it through the crystal stone of love. I love poetry and I love the night:

> She walks in beauty like the night,
> Of cloudless climes and starry skies,
> And all that is best of dark and bright,
> Meet in her aspect and her eyes.

I have started thinking about the mystery of quantum mechanics. It really is a strange theory. And I cannot understand the role of probabilities in it. How does a single electron decide to take a particular path? Does it know what path other electrons have taken? Does it know probabilities? I do not believe it. There is something crazy in quantum mechanics that I cannot understand. Even Einstein could not understand it!

Shadows of Lost Time

I want to spend my life trying to understand why quantum mechanics is probabilistic and not deterministic. But Feynman has warned that anyone who tries to understand quantum mechanics is doomed to fail. Am I walking into darkness here? Will I ever see light? Will I spend my life trying to understand quantum mechanics without finding an answer?

But I *cannot* research anything else. Who am I researching for? Myself. To quench my own intellectual thirst; a thirst that can never be quenched and that will lead to greater thirst.

Why should I listen to Feynman? Why should I listen to anyone? I will follow my own path. Success and failure do not matter. I must take my own road. Is that not bravery? The only bravery?

I have started writing a series of articles on science called *Veritas*. *Veritas* in Latin means truth. Through these articles, I want to share my excitement about science with others. I will put you on my e-mailing list.

Love,
Kanwar

Dear Anju, Dear Olga

6th January, 1942

Dear Olga,

Have you ever seen the ground covered with red snow? It looks beautiful if you forget that it is stained red with blood. Thousands of people die here every day. The lucky ones are killed instantly by the shells. The rest die of hunger, their bodies withering as their minds feel each painful moment of that slow death. So slow, that you are nauseated by the waiting.

When you are hungry, time passes slowly. We eat our ration of bread in two minutes and then we wait for the next 23 hours and 58 minutes for the next day's share. Each minute is an eternity. I wish I was able to sleep so that those waiting hours will pass more quickly. But even in sleep I dream of food. A bite of food is all that I need to make me happy. I have no sense of taste left. I just need to eat something.

Anna and I lie on the bed all day and night. It stinks, our clothes stink. But it does not bother us. The bodies of people lying outside on the road do not bother us. We just wait for food.

I cannot think about anything except food. I do not care about Tolstoy or Dostoevsky or Marx or God. I do not even care about the Madman. Let him eat the world. Just give me a bite of bread and I will worship anyone. Make me a slave but give me a bite of bread. I will sell my body, my mind, my hopes for one piece of bread.

Yesterday, I tried to boil my old shoes. We made them really soft. Not much came out of that. We are hungry. We are tired. We want to die.

Yours,
Yakov

14th December, 2000

Dear Anju,

Marriage is beautiful. And Jasmeen is a wonderful wife. She has added so much happiness to my life that I feel blessed. She has a really beautiful heart full of affection. And guess what, she makes such wonderful *biryani*. Lip-smacking! You have to taste it.

Yesterday, Jasmeen and I had a long discussion about beliefs. She is quite a religious person. That will change soon as the Age of Reason descends upon her. I told her that I really do not believe in anything. She was quite surprised. Rather, she was shocked. But then I told her about the idea of scepticism and how it is at the root of the scientific method and that in science all belief is understood to be provisional. A single experiment can prove a theory wrong, but even a million experiments cannot prove it right. We scientists bow only to the sublime power of the scientific method. Even the facts of science do not deserve our reverence. The great scientists of the past should not be revered. Understood, yes! Revered, No! Never! In effect, I told her that the only thing worth believing in is the power of disbelief.

Love,
Kanwar

27th January, 1942

Dear Olga,

Anna is dead. She died this morning while walking with me to get our daily ration of bread. She was too weak. She was too hungry. She just collapsed on the road and died. She did not look like Anna. She looked like a skeleton.

I looked at her for a minute and then I began walking again. I did not even feel guilty. I just kept walking. I could not think of anything but food.

When I got my bread, I wolfed it down and felt better. After that I felt guilty that I had left my precious Anna alone on the cold, wet road. On my way back, I sat next to her and wept. Her hand felt like ice. Her eyes had lost their warmth. She was dead. Dead and so terribly cold. I will never see her again. I will never see her smile again. I will never feel her touch again.

And then I went home and lay down on the stinking bed waiting for the next morning when I will get bread again. My mind was full of a dismal sense of time. It is time that I mourned, and not Anna's death.

I have become an animal. I cannot think of anything except food. I have no other desires in life. I just want to eat a piece of bread. Just one.

These letters are my only connection left with my humanity; a human being who once wondered about life, about the universe, who used to write about the joy of thinking. Today, all that remains is a hungry animal. Why did I write so much? Why did I not pass my time eating then? Why do I live?

A miserable little animal,
Yakov

15th April, 2010

Dear Anju,

Life is wonderful with Jasmeen and the kids. The kids really keep us busy all day. They are so curious about everything. It is almost incredible. Yesterday, Sidak asked me about the maximum number that one can count. That was a perfect time to introduce the concept of infinity to him. I told him that four things are infinite: space, time, numbers and the human mind.

It is almost unbelievable the extent to which a human mind can imagine and think, and how much we have evolved from animal instincts. We think so little about our needs at the most basic level: food, sex, shelter. Most of our thoughts are about more abstract ideas or feelings: love, self–esteem, respect, glory, pride. And some of us reach even higher, to exalted spheres such as art, music, science, poetry. I really want my children to grow up to look at life from the highest plane of thought. I want them to live surrounded by ephemeral ideas. I want them to cherish knowledge. I want them to grow up to value their thoughts and imagination. It is the needs of the mind and not the body that should be the core of our values and our lives.

Curiouser and curiouser,
Kanwar

Sometime in March, 1942

Dear Olga,

Life has been sucked out of my body. I am a walking skeleton. I no longer have the desire to walk to the ration kiosk for my bread. I want to die. I will never see you again. I will never see Sasha and Gregory.
We will never laugh together again. Or run on those green fields or joke about Papa's cap.
I will hold your picture and sleep now. And I will keep that book beside me. Perhaps someone will read it

one day and know who Yakov Perelman was. Perhaps someday my highest self will manifest as a spark of curiosity in the mind of a child. Then, I will live again. Today I will die.

Yakov

17th June, 2010

Dear Anju,

    I will tell you about something very sad. I don't know if you know about the Siege of Leningrad. It was the bloodiest siege in history. Over two million people died, most of them of starvation because the Germans had cut off all food supplies. In a speech in Munich, Hitler had said: "Leningrad must perish by starvation". He really was a madman. The siege lasted for 870 days. Imagine 870 days of hunger!
    But the body dies, the ideas of the mind do not die. They are passed on and live again in the mind of another.
    Last night, I was talking about the books that have influenced me the most in life. You know how Jasmeen, Kavita and I have discussions at the dinner table. One of those books is *Physics Can Be Fun*. It was the book that sparked curiosity in my mind when I was a thirteen-year-old boy. Do you remember the experiments that I used to show you from this book?

Dear Anju, Dear Olga

After everyone went to bed, I decided to look up the author on the internet: the man who had inspired me to think beyond the small needs of life, and led me into the haloed world of scientific thinking. And this is what I discovered. In 1942, during the siege of Leningrad in the Second World War, Yakov Perelman died of starvation.

The man who taught me the joys of the mind died of hunger. The mind can race to the farthest boundaries of the universe but it must still depend on the body for nourishment. All nourishment had been denied to the wonderful mind of Yakov Perelman. I wish he could come to my door. I would see that he was never hungry again.

Yakov's spirit lives on in the curiosity he aroused in my mind and in the minds of thousands of others who have read and been inspired by his books.

And my children will read his books and carry forward that spirit of curiosity.

Kanwar

Was Xanthippe a Shrew?

Two men are seated across a table in the popular Big Chill café in Khan Market in Delhi. They have just finished eating a delicious meal of lamb chops, fish in red wine sauce, and are now finishing their cheesecake. A book lies on the table between them and they both refer to it from time to time. The two men have been discussing subjects of an abstract nature and both seem to have enjoyed the discussion very much.

Russell: That was a delightful meal, Mr. Grewal. I have spoken about philosophers who forgot their meals or read a book while eating. Thankfully, we are not like them. Is it not satisfying to enjoy the pleasures of the body while indulging in the pleasures of the mind? We have had a wonderful meal and have enjoyed the discussion as well. Coming back to our topic, what were we talking about?

Grewal: You were saying something about Xanthippe.

Was Xanthippe a Shrew?

Russell: Oh, yes! Xanthippe was a shrew.

Just then three men and a woman enter the café. All three men have beards. Two of them are bald. All of them are wearing cloaks that seem to be from a different age. The oldest man is quite ugly; bald, short and unkempt. The woman is very beautiful and looks very young. The other bald man is quite tall and broad and seems to wear a permanent frown on his face. The third man is handsome and well built.

Waiter: How many people, sir?

Tall bald man: Table for four please. Do you have lower seats for women?

The woman looks at him angrily. She wants to say something nasty but stops herself.

Waiter: Whose name will it be in?

Tall bald man: Plato. Oh, I am sorry! The pupil should always put the master first. Make that Socrates.

The short, ugly, bald man smiles. They are given a table very close to the one where Mr. Russell and Mr. Grewal are seated.

Russell: Mr. Grewal, I have a feeling that we will enjoy listening to these people talk. Shall we order coffee and stay for a little while longer? I know that it is quite ungentlemanly to eavesdrop but in this particular case, I am willing to make an exception.

Mr. Grewal nods his head in agreement and orders coffee. Mr. Russell and Mr. Grewal discover that the woman's name is Xanthippe and the handsome man answers to the name of Xenophon.

Plato [*angrily*]: Why are we here? My study of perfect forms has been interrupted by this. Is this your doing, Xanthippe? What exactly is your problem?

Xanthippe: This has gone on for too long. For over 2300 years I have been called a shrew by just about anyone who reads your *Dialogues* or reads the biography of Socrates. It is time we discussed some things and set the record straight. Whenever someone uses the name Xanthippe and shrew in the same sentence, my blood boils. [*Turns and looks towards Socrates*] I said to myself that when this happened for the 10,000th time, I would bring you all back on earth and tell this Plato guy what I really think of him and his *Dialogues* and for putting my name in such bad light. Today happens to be the 10,000th time and we are all back together to talk about some things. Do you know that they have even named a species of shrew after me; Xanthippe's shrew? That is disgusting. You have caused all this, Plato!

Plato [*grinning*]: What is the scientific name of Xanthippe's shrew?

Was Xanthippe a Shrew?

Xanthippe: *Crocidura xantippe*. It is found in the dry shrub lands of Kenya and Tanzania.

Xenophon: You are not a shrew, you are just the most beautiful woman in all of Greece.

Plato: Xenophon, it is not proper to talk about your master's wife like that. Besides, she is not a perfect beauty. Perfect beauty is the idea of beauty, and that is only possible in God's heaven. Everything on earth is a mere copy, an imperfect copy, of that perfection. And everything on earth, since it is impure, also has a degree of ugliness. Therefore, Xanthippe is a mixture of the beautiful and ugly. In this respect, she is like all things that are worldly.

Socrates: I thought that I was supposed to say all this.

Plato: You say all these things in my *Dialogues*. In reality, I say all these things.

Socrates: Xanthippe, I do not understand what you hope to achieve today. Why have you brought us all here? You did nag me a lot and argue a lot, which is why people call you a shrew. And even if we prove today that you are not a shrew, how will you remove the association of the word shrew with the name Xanthippe from people's minds?

Shadows of Lost Time

Xanthippe: Yes, I argued a lot. I thought you liked arguments. I thought that you were all for the "Socratic method" of finding the truth. You even gave it a fancy name, *elenchus*. But when I show you the truth by arguing, you do not seem to appreciate it at all.

Socrates: It is *elenchus* when I am winning. Otherwise it is a useless argument caused by nagging people.

Xanthippe [*smiling*]: So you accept that you never won a philosophical argument with me?

Before Socrates can speak, Plato interjects.

Plato: The great master does not wish to argue with shrews.

Xanthippe: I really have to teach you a lesson, Plato. But first, let me call someone who can permanently erase the connection between my name and the word shrew, though I must admit that he caused a lot of damage to my reputation by comparing me with a shrew in his works. He will have to fix that. Just a second.

Xanthippe calls someone on her mobile phone.

Xanthippe: He says that he will be here in about fifteen minutes.

Was Xanthippe a Shrew?

Plato [*in a sing-song tone*]: You are a shrew. You are a shrew. You are a shrew.

Xanthippe [*visibly annoyed but controlling herself*]: Plato, you said that all knowledge is recall.

Plato: Yes, I have discussed this topic at length in *Meno* and *Phaedo*. All true knowledge is eternal. The soul is immortal. Therefore the soul knows everything. However, all knowledge is forgotten with the pain of birth. And then, during the life of the person, it may be remembered. So, all learning is recall of what is already known, eternally known. I call this *anamnesis*.

Xanthippe [*smiles*]: Do you recall what I will do now?

Plato: Umm, uh.... No! I forget.

Xanthippe folds a newspaper and hits it hard on Plato's head.

Plato: Ouch!

Xanthippe: I wanted to do this so that by shaking your brains, you are able to recall a bit more. Now tell me what I am going to do now.

Plato [*rubbing his head*]: How do I know?

Xanthippe: Exactly!

She hits the newspaper on Plato's head again, this time a lot harder.

Plato: Hey! That hurt.

Xanthippe: You forget very fast. Your powers of recall are indeed poor.

Xenophon cannot control his laughter.

Xenophon: Ha! Ha! Ha! I like this kind of philosophical discussion. Let's name it *whackelenchus*! Ha! Ha! What a treat. What a woman!

Socrates: Beware of her, Plato! She does these things all the time. Do you remember, she once poured a bucket of water over me just outside my house when I was meditating on a philosophical topic?

Plato: I remember.

Xanthippe: That is just a part of the story and quite inaccurate as well. Let me tell you the whole thing now.

Socrates: Can we *not* talk about this?

Xanthippe: Yes, we will!

Plato: She really is a shrew!

Was Xanthippe a Shrew?

Xanthippe: Once, I heard Soc discussing a topic with his... er... friend, Alcibiades. Soc told him about absolute justice, absolute good and absolute beauty, and how these can be understood only by pure intellectual thought and not by our bodies. He told Alcibiades that there is a difference between knowledge and opinion. He said that knowledge can only be about things that are eternal and, therefore, can only be understood by the soul. Opinion is about things that are not eternal; things that our bodies feel or see or experience.

Plato: Master, why were you saying all this to Alcibiades? He was not very philosophical. In fact, he was not even liberally endowed with brains.

Xanthippe: He just wanted to impress Alcibiades! Alcibiades was very handsome, you know. And these were not Soc's original ideas. I knew that he had been getting this stuff from you, Plato. Therefore, I decided to confront him. I told him that though there are some things that one can only know by pure intellectual thought, there are many others which one cannot. For scientific knowledge one needs to collect observations and then form knowledge. And observations can only be collected by the senses. So the senses do aid us in the formation of knowledge. There is nothing evil in seeing and feeling the world around you, and it only expands one's thinking. I told him that knowledge is not recollection. It is the collection of facts and the formation of patterns out of those facts.

Plato: I know your crazy thoughts. You are a hardcore empiricist and physicalist. But what did the exalted master say to your nonsense?

Xenophon [*excited*]: I am a physicalist too. In fact everyone in the army is a physicalist. Physical violence, physical...

Plato: Xenophon. We are not talking about that. Physicalism is a philosophical concept. Please relax. Xanthippe, tell me what Socrates said about your nonsense?

Xanthippe: He could not say anything. He did not have you there. So he could not answer my questions. He would have had to ask you the answer. And then I told him that he married me because he found me beautiful. And I told him that he seeks Alcibiades because he is handsome. Therefore, he cannot reject the senses and talk about the soul but still spend all his energy seeking beautiful people and trying to impress them with matters that they cannot understand, even if they lived for a thousand years. And then, my dear husband went into one of his world famous trances. He just stood there as if meditating about something spiritual. He really can do that for hours. I always knew that he had perfected the art of going into trances so that he could avoid arguments when they become uncomfortable for him. I decided that I needed to puncture the bubble of his trance and at the same time show that the senses can bring one's thoughts right back to where they should be – in the world around us.

Xenophon: Then what did you do?

Xanthippe: I poured a bucket of icy cold water on his head. He came right back and shouted at me. The water proved several things: Soc just acts those trances; he avoids uncomfortable discussions by using those trances; the body, and what it feels, can bring the mind to its earthly state; cold water is an eternal tool to break all trances and dreams and, therefore, it is a Platonic form. Right, Mr. Plato?

Socrates stares across the room at a pretty girl and goes into a trance.

Xanthippe: See, he does it again.

Xenophon: But why was he trying to impress Alcibiades?

Xanthippe: Because Soc is a gay.

Xenophon: I know that the master is happy. You say he is gay. That is just tautology.

Plato [*surprised that Xenophon knows the meaning of tautology[1]*]: No. All gay men are not happy and not all those who are happy are gay.

Xenophon: I cannot understand. I use syllogisms[2] to understand everything. Let's try this:
    Major Premise: All happy men are gay.
    Minor Premise: Socrates is a happy man.
    Conclusion: Socrates is gay.
See, it is so simple to understand now.

Xanthippe: Your conclusions are correct but your premises are not. Why don't you stick to the one example of syllogism that you actually know, the one related to Socrates being mortal.

Xenophon: Yes. We should start from there. All men are mortal. Socrates is a man. Therefore...

Socrates [*waking up from his trance*]: Enough! I am sick of people using the example of me being mortal to illustrate syllogisms. And they have been doing it for over 2300 years. I am tired of it.

Xanthippe: You are sick of being used in a syllogism? My name has been synonymous with a shrew for the same number of years. How do you think I feel about that?

Was Xanthippe a Shrew?

Socrates, Plato and Xenophon look at Xanthippe, and perhaps for the first time, understand her annoyance at being the definition of a shrewish wife.

Xanthippe: And you, Plato, prevented my book *The Second Sex* from being published. It would have started a wave of feminism. In fact, the second wave of feminism would have occurred before the first wave.[3] I am glad that someone eventually did write the book. But it happened too late, 2200 years after I first had the idea. How beautifully the book highlights the existentialist idea *existence precedes essence* with the statement, "One is not born a woman, but becomes one".

Socrates: What is existentialism?[3] Never heard of anything with that name.

Plato: Your views on the rights of women would have been dangerous to my *Republic*, Xanthippe. I had given a great place to women in my *Republic*. What more does one need?

Xanthippe: The state selecting the person that you should marry. Is that a great idea? The state following the principles of eugenics[4] to improve offspring. Great idea? No! Taking children from mothers so that they belong to the state. Another great idea? No! These are terrible ideas. Have you never heard of love or human affection?

Xenophon [*excited*]: Would there be free sex too? I am starting to like the *Republic* already!

Plato: Love is a weakness of the body. The only real and true love is the love for knowledge and that too, the love for philosophy. For the state, one must have duties. And the duty of citizens is to live according to the laws of the *Republic* and obey the Philosopher-Kings.

Xanthippe: What is philosophy, Plato?

Xenophon [*eagerly*]: I know. I know. I learnt the definition once. Philosophy is a field of study that is intermediate between...ummm...hmm. How can I forget?!

Plato: Philosophy is what I define in my *Dialogues* and the *Republic*.

Xanthippe: Then you are the worst philosopher ever! You try to prevent others from questioning. You decide what to call philosophy and what to call trash and then you expect future philosophers to follow you. You want philosophers that come after you to follow you without questioning. That is not philosophy. Philosophy is to question. Philosophy is to reason. Philosophy is to discuss. Right, Soc?

Socrates: I have to think about it [*seems to go into a trance*].

Was Xanthippe a Shrew?

Xanthippe: You seem to be going around in circles, Plato. You contradict yourself. Your concept of philosophy is different from what you want others to follow. Soc has no such problems. He never goes around in circles. He just lies on his bed or goes into a trance and resolves all contradictions instantly [*smiles*].

Xenophon [*proudly*]: I, too, never seem to face contradictions.

Plato: That is because you are not capable of thinking two thoughts at once. Therefore, no contradictions, Xeno.

Xanthippe: And yours was the first of many Utopias that have been proposed. All of them have failed. In fact, many countries and rulers throughout history have tried to implement parts of your *Republic*. They all failed miserably. You should have listened to me and incorporated my feedback. But, instead, you called me a shrew!

Plato [*angry*]: My ideas a failure? Never! Are you trying to imply that I was a fool not to have listened to your gibberish? No. Never. Xenophon, a fool? Definitely. Socrates, a fool, quite likely! But I am the greatest philosopher ever.

Socrates [*wakes up from his trance at being called a fool*]: *Et tu, Plato*[5]?

Shadows of Lost Time

Plato [*loudly*]: Your statement is ahead of its time Socrates. And the language is not ours either. You speak Julie's language who came after us.

Socrates is taken aback at the lack of respect shown by Plato. Plato realises his mistake.

Plato [*politely*]: Your statement is ahead of its time, O exalted master. The words of a barbarian emperor who will come after us do not suit your divine tongue.

A man with a moustache and a large frill around his neck enters the room. Mr. Russell is quite surprised but hides it and bows slightly.

Xanthippe: My dear Bard of Avon[6]. We have been waiting for you.

Bard of Avon:

> Like him that travels I return again,
> Just to the time, not with the time exchanged.

Socrates: Who is this and why does he talk so strangely. And what language?

Plato: He is an English poet. It is a Germanic language and in some ways even more vulgar than Vulgar Latin[7]. He was the guy who said something like *all the world's a stage, and all men and women merely players*.

Was Xanthippe a Shrew?

Socrates: Is he any good?

Plato: He is very popular but I personally do not like him. Poets that write about love, passion and jealousy are not good for the *Republic*. I prefer poets that write about heroism and national pride. Also, this man is a playwright. I had decided to banish all dramatists from my *Republic* for in every drama there are villains and they can corrupt the minds of the citizens.

Xanthippe: You talk about only reading poets of heroism and avoiding poets that write about passion! But do you know what your master reads when his... er... friend Alcibiades is around. Have a look under Soc's mattress sometime, Plato, and you will find out.

Socrates tries to go into a trance but a slap on his hand from Xanthippe prevents this luxury.

Xanthippe: Bard of Avon, you have done great damage to my reputation. Plato called me a shrew first but I do not think many people read Plato anymore. You called me a shrew in your play *The Taming of the Shrew* and because of that my name has been forever associated with shrews. And people read you a lot. You should have been more careful not to trust a person like Plato. He is very good at making up stories.

Shadows of Lost Time

Bard of Avon:

> If we shadows have offended,
> Think but this, and all is mended,
> That you have but slumber'd here
> While these visions did appear
> And this weak and idle theme,
> No more yielding but a dream,
> Gentles, do not reprehend:
> If you pardon, we will mend.

Xenophon scratches his head for he cannot understand a single word.

Xanthippe: Can you repeat what you said about me in *The Taming of the Shrew*.

Bard of Avon:

> Be she as foul as was Florentius' love,
> As old as Sibyl, and as curst and shrewd
> As Socrates' Xanthippe or a worse,
> She moves me not, or not removes, at least,
> Affection's edge in me, were she as rough
> As are the swelling Adriatic seas.

Plato giggles. Socrates tries not to look ignorant. Xenophon does not even try.

Was Xanthippe a Shrew?

Xanthippe: You will have to correct all this, Mr. Bard of Avon. I want you to write a play that is historically correct and presents the philosophy of Plato, and my philosophy, accurately and without any prejudice. And Soc has to be represented as a silly husband who listens to others more than his own wife and who is unwilling to accept that his wife can be infinitely smarter than him. A male chauvinist pig! And you can portray Xenophon as a cute but silly chap who is very fond of me. Is that too much to ask, Mr. Bard of Avon?

Xenophon: Xanthippe. My dear Xanthippe.

Bard of Avon:

> No, madam; so it stead you, I will write
> Please you command, a thousand times as much;
> And yet--

Plato: Xenophon may be "cute" but he is so innocent of philosophy. Why do you bother with him?

Xanthippe: Did you notice that he opened the door for me when we entered the restaurant? Soc did not do that in 2300 years. Xenophon may be lacking philosophically, and he may be lacking in all aspects that are attributable to the brain, but he is good natured and respects women.

Socrates [*jealously*]: Xanthippe. How can you talk like this about him in front of me?

Xanthippe: Don't worry Soc. My feelings for him are strictly... er... platonic.

Plato smiles.

Socrates: But my feelings for you are...well... Socratic.

Xanthippe: And that means going into a trance to avoid any argument in which your wife seems to have the upper hand.

Plato: He only opened the door for you. What is the big deal about that?

Xanthippe: It is better than having the doors of history closed on you and your thoughts forever by your own husband and his pupil.

Xenophon: And guess what? Both of our names begin with X. X for Xenophon and X for Xanthippe.

Plato giggles again. Socrates looks disgusted.

Xanthippe: Silly but cute.

Bard of Avon:

    Farewell, my dearest sister, fare thee well:

Was Xanthippe a Shrew?

> The elements be kind to thee, and make
> Thy spirits all of comfort! fare thee well.

Plato : Farewell, O funny sounding Bard of Avon.

Bard of Avon:

> And whether we shall meet again I know not.
> Therefore our everlasting farewell take.
> Forever, and forever, farewell, Cassius!
> If we do meet again, why, we shall smile;
> If not, why then this parting was well made.

The Bard of Avon gets up and walks towards the door. Mr. Russell bows respectfully.

Plato: Let's not bother with the Bard of Avon or any other Bard of any other place. Let me offer you a deal. A fantastic deal. I will rewrite my *Dialogues* but this time I will give an honest and proper place to you and your thoughts. And if you want, we can even make Socrates...umm... the exalted master, go into his trances a few times. Divine heavenly trances. What do you say?

Xanthippe: You cannot write about my philosophy.

Plato: Why not?

Xenophon [*smiling dreamily*]: X X. x x. X x. x X.

Xanthippe: Because you do not understand it.

Plato [*astonished*]: I do not understand your philosophy?

Xanthippe: Yes, my dear Plato. You are a lesser philosopher than me and, therefore, you cannot write about my philosophy. A modern philosopher by the name of Bertrand Russell wrote so beautifully in his book *The History of Western Philosophy:*

A stupid man's report of what a clever man says can never be accurate, because he unconsciously translates what he hears into something he can understand. I would rather be reported by my bitterest enemy among philosophers than a friend innocent of philosophy.

Mr. Russell smiles, picks up *The History of Western Philosophy* that has been lying on the table between them throughout the meal, and puts it in his bag as Mr. Grewal asks for the bill.

[**Apologies to the ancient masters and their pupils**]

Was Xanthippe a Shrew?

Socrates was one of the founders of Western philosophy. Plato, a classical Greek philosopher, and Xenophon, historian and soldier, were his students.

Socrates did not write any books. Plato's Dialogues *have Socrates as the hero but historians suspect that much of the philosophy attributed to Socrates is actually Plato's own. So we do not know much about Socrates except from Plato's writings.*

Xanthippe was Socrates' wife and William Shakespeare refers to her as a shrew in his play The Taming of the Shrew.

---

[1] Tautology in Greek means same word/idea i.e. to say the same thing in two different ways. Tautology adds nothing to an argument and is considered a fault of style in speech or writing.

[2] Syllogisms are the oldest form of logical inference and appear in Plato's *Dialogues*. The syllogism related to Socrates is the most commonly used example.

[3] *The Second Sex* by Simone de Beauvoir started what is known as the second wave of feminism (the first wave began in the 19th century). Simone de Beauvoir was a close friend of Jean-Paul Sartre, the 20th century existentialist philosopher.

[4] The act of choosing parents to improve offspring is known as eugenics. This was one of the proposals in Plato's *Republic*.

[5] *Et tu, Brutus* are supposedly the last words spoken by the Roman emperor Julius Caesar to his friend Marcus Brutus in 44 BC.

[6] William Shakespeare.

[7] Latin was the language of the Romans. Vulgar Latin was spoken by the common man. French originates from Vulgar Latin, English is a Germanic language.

A Story Hidden in the Depths

Mary had not written a single word in the last year and a half. She had written more than fifteen short stories before that but over the last eighteen months, as she sat at the table in her study with a pen in her hand, an immense blankness filled her mind that was mirrored in the sheets of pristine white paper that lay in front of her. She yearned for that one story that would define her and make her fall in love with her own writing. When she thought of all the stories she had written, they seemed to her to be superficial, almost frivolous. She would gladly give them all up in exchange for one story that really expressed who she was and what she wanted to say. But how does one search for a creative idea? Perhaps she needed some time alone, away from the bustle of Chicago; a month at a place where her friends and overbearing family would not find her. And what better place for a month of solitude than a cruise on a ship? A long voyage on the ocean would relax her and help her to find stories from the depths of her own heart. She hoped that she would be able to discover the voices of her soul, voices that were overpowered by the noise of the people and life that surrounded her at home.

So Mary had optimistically embarked on a cruise of the Atlantic. Once on board, she had spent her days searching for ideas in the faces of men and women on the ship but none inspired a story. She had stared for hours at the waves, hoping that inspiration would ride in on them. Days had become weeks as each evening she had forced herself to sit at the desk in her cabin holding a pen in her hand. An hour or so later, she would lie down on her bed without having written a single word. The voyage had not given her what she desired.

Now there was only one night left of her cruise. She had spent the evening walking on deck, pacing back and forth, dejected at having wasted money and an entire month on a journey that had not yielded even one story, let alone the special one she craved.

To mark the end of the cruise, the captain had arranged a party. As darkness descended upon the sea, the passengers came out on deck to enjoy their final night on the ship. Mary did not want to join in, she felt incompetent and morose. She decided to walk back to her cabin and when she reached it, she lay down on her bunk. She could hear loud music and the revelry only made her feel worse. She was annoyed by the music, by the ship and its passengers and, most of all, she was annoyed with herself. She wondered how the others partied day and night without feeling that their time had been wasted. They have shallow minds, she said to herself. But then she wondered what she had achieved. Just like the others,

A Story Hidden in the Depths

she had squandered her days on the ship but, unlike her fellow passengers, she had not even managed to gain any pleasure from her cruise. So maybe they had not wasted their days, after all. They had come to have fun and they had been successful at it. But she felt like a failure. How long would she keep writing silly college romances? She wanted to write a story that moved hearts. When would she write something worthwhile? Tears wet Mary's cheeks as she lay there thinking of her wasted journey.

Mary switched off the light and tried to sleep. She imagined the immense ocean that surrounded her as she lay only meters above its infinite depths and wondered at the untold secrets that were hidden there. If only the ocean would share one of its mysteries with her, only one of the millions that are locked in its heart.

"Tell me your story!" she cried out loud. "Just tell me one of your stories," she pleaded.

As soon as she uttered these words, an eerie quiet descended upon the room. She could not hear the music from the deck. Mary became still as the silence engulfed her. Then she froze as she heard a soft rustling sound.

"I will tell you my story," whispered a voice. "Today, you will hear a story that will move hearts."

Although this strange, soft voice in her room did not frighten her, Mary was unable to move or to speak; unable to ask the voice who he was and why he had come to her. As though reading her mind, the voice continued:

"My name is Jem. I was given that name by the people who brought me away from my home in Africa. They gave me this name because my original African name was too difficult for them to pronounce. I hated it. They told me that I was to be sent to a wonderful new place. I did not believe them. I knew I was merely a slave to them, useful and nothing more."

As Mary listened, the voice grew powerful. Although he spoke calmly, Mary sensed deep pain as Jem told his story.

"Africa! How I loved my country! I grew up fishing on Lake Debo with my father who was the chief of the Bozo fishermen. Bozos were the masters of the Niger River. Every year we would wait for it to flood and fill the lake. The river never failed us. It was a beautiful life, full of happiness. My father and I would catch fish during the day for my mother to cook for the evening meal. After we had eaten, I would sit beside my parents and we would sing together. The cool breeze off the lake would make our sleep pleasant and refresh us when we woke in the morning. I felt as though nothing could ever go wrong in my world. My parents and the sparkling lake was my life. My most beautiful seventeen years were spent there.

'But greed has no end and no religion. One day, I had been out fishing alone and as I returned to my village at dusk, I was captured by the Nagalu tribe, along with the rest of my people. Only the old were left behind. The rest of us were marched to the sea on a journey that lasted several days. We walked with our hands tied behind our backs. We were given very little food and just allowed a few hours of rest each day. My father tried to resist and was cruelly beaten. I never knew what happened to my mother, I never saw her again.

A Story Hidden in the Depths

'When we reached the coast, we were split into groups and sold to white men. My father tried to stay with me but he was pushed away and sold to different white men far from where I stood. I cannot forget the look in his eyes as he was separated from me. I was bought by British slave traders for two bottles of rum and a musket and these new masters gave me the name Jem. They pushed me and the others in my group onto a boat and then aboard a ship. That evening, I wept as we set sail away from my beautiful world. I longed to see my mother and father, to go back to the lake and fish again. But I felt in my heart that I would never see my parents or my home again. I prayed for my mother, I prayed that she was at peace, that she would never be unhappy. But my heart broke when I imagined how my parents were suffering, not knowing where I was. I wanted to tell them that, wherever I went, I would always think of them. I spoke to the wind and begged it to take my message to them. I knew that they would recognize my voice when they heard it on the breeze. "

Mary's eyes filled with tears. She knew no words to offer comfort for such loss so she lay there in her dark cabin listening to the voice that had become heavy with pain and misery.

"The white men had given the ship a funny name: *Zong*! I was taken to the hold of that ship. It was a horrible and terrifying place. I had never seen so many people crammed into such a small space. All around me were hopeless, frightened faces. A sickening stench made me retch. I wished at that moment that I had never been born.

'I was shackled to another man, my right wrist and ankle tied to his left wrist and ankle. The white man who brought us there then left us and went back up to the clean air on deck. I cannot convey the misery of that first night as I sat and waited, bound by rope to a stranger. I think we were waiting for something to happen, something that would end this nightmare, and we would magically wake up from a bad dream. I did not sleep that night, my mind full of fear and anger at the terrible conditions that we were kept in. It was pitch dark inside the hold, I could not even see my own hands in front of me. After a few hours, as my companion dropped off to sleep, his weight pulled painfully against the ropes around my wrist. I did not want to wake him from the oblivion of sleep so I sat on, sickened by the awful smell and trying to block out the sound of voices groaning in pain.

'The morning brought something so welcome: a beam of light entered the hold. I did not know of any way to avoid this terrible fate but that ray of light seemed to inspire a little hope in my heart. As I gazed at the dust moats dancing in the golden haze, I saw her. She had the most beautiful face that I had ever seen and eyes that made me think of Lake Debo at dawn: warm, soft and endless. She seemed sad and almost resigned to her fate. She looked at me for a moment and then turned her eyes away. But that one moment shook my soul. I wanted to go to her and protect her from everything that is bad in this world. I continued to stare at her but then the row of people in front of her shifted position and she was hidden from my sight.

'At that moment some white men entered the hold. They were carrying food and gave each of us a little bowl of rice and yam to eat. It was not enough. As soon as they had left, some of the slaves tried to snatch their neighbour's rations and a few scuffles broke out over these tiny bowls of food.

'My companion had slept through this so I woke him up and gave him his share of rice and yam. He thanked me and started to cry as he hungrily devoured his meagre rations. Afterwards, he started to tell me about himself. His name was Alik. He was older than me and had been recently married. Only a few days after his marriage, he and his wife were captured and brought with the others of his tribe to the coast for sale. His wife had been taken on board another ship and he had no idea where that ship was bound. They almost certainly would never meet again. He was heartbroken.

'Days became nights and nights turned into days. The foul smell only grew worse and quarrels among the slaves broke out more frequently. Disease spread. Many died after vomiting blood, their bodies consumed by the filth and disease around them. The captain of the ship was worried.

'To pass the endless days, I spoke with those around me and learned that every slave sold in Jamaica earned the company a lot of money. We thought that this meant that the captain would do his best to save us. I got the impression that the white men were relieved that some of us had died because it freed up more space for the rest of us. And there would also be more food to go round. In an effort to keep us healthy, the captain ordered that we were to be taken on deck in batches for an hour of fresh air and exercise each day.

'At least we had something to look forward to, that one hour of clean, sweet air on deck. But somehow it made the return to the filthy, stinking hold packed with men and women even harder to bear.

'And then, several days later, I saw her again. Alik and I were climbing the ladder to the deck for our exercise and she was being brought back to the hold. I smiled as our eyes met. She smiled back. I would have given up a hundred trips to the deck for that one moment. Hope rose in my heart again. I thought about her all day. By evening, I had decided to look for her and talk to her. I knew that she may not want to talk to me but I had to try. But finding her and talking to her would be difficult among the bodies packed in the hold. Because of the lack of space, many of us had to sleep sitting up. Even so, I would try in the morning and I smiled happily at the thought. Others looked at me and thought that I had gone mad. They were right.

'The next morning I woke up with the thought that today is the day when I will go and talk to her. But how would I convince Alik? Why would Alik want to move through the crowd of groaning people and risk falling over? Maybe I could offer him something in return. What? I had nothing. When Alik woke up I gave him two bowls of food. He looked surprised but also delighted to see the unexpected extra serving of rice and yam. He did not ask any questions and began gobbling it up. When he had finished, he told me that he had known that the captain would increase our rations because he did not want any more slaves to die. He smiled and looked around him. He was surprised to see that the others still had only one bowl each and he looked back at me questioningly. I told him that I had given him my share because I wanted him to walk with me to find the girl. He laughed. It was the first time I had seen him laugh. Then, abruptly, he stopped laughing and tears came into his eyes. He told me that I did not need to give him my food, that he knew what love is and would gladly help me find her. I was delighted. I had something to look forward to now.

'That day, after our allotted time on deck, Alik and I walked among the closely packed men and women in the hold. Some glared at us as we jostled them and Alik would stare angrily back at them. He was a big man and that prevented people from doing more than grumbling. And then I saw her. She looked at me and then angrily looked away. I went close to her and greeted her. She did not respond. I tried several times to speak to her but she would not look at me again. I felt sad as we walked back to our corner of the hold.

'In the evening Alik told me that love is not easy, that one had to try really hard to win it. For the first time since our voyage began, I saw excitement in Alik's eyes. He had become my friend. For several days after that,

Alik and I would push our way slowly through the crowd to the part of the hold where she sat. She never spoke to us. She would just look away. I began to feel dejected. But every evening as we sat together, Alik would inspire me with stories of love and advice on what I should do or say. But nothing seemed to help.

'One evening Alik told me his own story, how he had given a shell necklace to a girl in a nearby village and how that gift made her fall in love with him. It seemed so simple: I thought, give her a gift and she will be mine. But what can a slave give another? I did not have a shell necklace to gift her. If she was in my village, I would have caught the biggest fish for her and she would have fallen in love with me. But now I was a slave who had nothing.

'The next morning Alik and I went to her again. I stood in front of her, not knowing what to say. And then I blurted out, 'I will die for you.' She looked up at me and started laughing, 'We are all going to die anyway. Sit down'. I felt incredibly happy. I sat there and told her about my village and my mother and the fish in our lake. She watched me silently with a smile on her face. And then she asked me to come back again the next day. That request lit up my heart. I did not want to die for her. I wanted to live for her.

'From then on, Alik and I would go to meet her every day. She told me about her life and she would laugh and talk so much when we were together. Her name was Asari. Alik would look the other way when Asari and I spoke to each other but I knew that he was listening to us.

A Story Hidden in the Depths

I think that he was happy because our conversations reminded him of his wife. Sometimes he would shake his head after I had finished speaking, as though he thought that I had said something stupid. But Asari would never make me feel stupid. She would keep looking at me with her divine eyes. We were only able to meet for an hour everyday when some of the slaves were on deck and it became easier to move around. One hour with her and the rest of the time spent thinking about her. I was happy. People were dying, conditions were miserable, but I was happy.

'Each day the hold was a little less crowded. Alik told me that more than fifty slaves had died since we had left Africa. He seemed to know so much. I think he knew the white men's language and listened to them when we were on deck. Some of the white men, too, had died of disease.

'I was friendly with some of the other slaves on the ship. But there was one, Chima, I did not like. He sat close to Asari and once, he had tried to touch her when she was sleeping at night. She had woken up and shouted at him. The next day someone changed places with Chima so that he was forced to sit far away from Asari. After that, whenever I met Asari, Chima would watch us with anger contorting his face. He seemed jealous of Asari's fondness for me.

'I would speak to Asari and tell her how I imagined our life in Jamaica. One day, I told her how we would find work in the same sugarcane fields and then we would be able to talk to each other all day, side by side.

She smiled at me. Maybe we would even live in the same house and have a little garden of our own. I said that I would go and catch fish for her and she would wait for me at home. She would cook the fish and when we had finished our meal, we would lie down together and sing songs till daybreak. As I said this, tears flowed down her cheeks. She placed her hand on my face and caressed it. I felt wonderful. I felt that I would never be lonely again. Every loss, every pain had gone from my heart. Suddenly, Alik turned and hugged me with tears in his eyes. Alik's spontaneous expression of emotion brought our private moment to an abrupt end. Asari laughed and her merriment brought a grin to both our faces.

'That night I thought of my mother, how I wished she could meet Asari. I felt that she would have been so happy with the girl her son had found for himself."

For the first time since the story began, Mary smiled. She knew that the power of love can transform the lives and minds of people. She had written so much about love in her stories but she understood now that she had never been able to convey this power so intensely.

Jem continued:

"Seventy five days had passed since we had begun our journey. Each day brought greater hardship, disease and misery. Each morning, our white masters would toss more dead bodies overboard, bodies of slaves who suffocated to death at night, or whose lives had been painfully drained by disease. We prayed that the dead were at peace, free from pain and suffering. Those left alive endured horror. Painful sores appeared on their bodies from being forced to remain in one position on the filthy floor. Our only hope was that each day brought us closer to our destination. Surely, the new life awaiting us would be better than this.

'I felt confident that I would make it through to the end of this voyage. I had not succumbed to disease and turned my thoughts away from the filth around me. I think it was my dreams of a happy life that sustained me and gave me strength. Maybe it was the blessings of my mother. I knew that, wherever she was, she was praying for me every day. Now, I would live for Asari. She called me by my new name, Jem, in such a beautiful and musical way that I started to like it. Asari seemed happier too. Once, she mischievously asked me if we should start thinking of names for our children.

'Then one day she became ill. For three days and nights her skin burned like hot coals. She lay still in her corner but would smile whenever she looked at me. I gave her my food and water. 'I will not die, Jem. I will live for you and for our children,' she said.

'On the eighty third day, something happened. The white men came as usual and we looked forward to our chance to be in the open air. But instead of gathering us together in small groups as they usually did, they looked carefully at each of us and took more than fifty slaves to the deck. They had been searching for the sick. At first we assumed that they had decided to give them more time in the fresh air to help them recover. But then we heard screams and the sickening splash of bodies hitting water. They were throwing them overboard.

'Why had the white men done this? Why kill us when each of us would fetch them more money? Surely it was worth their while to save as many of us as they could? Alik and I discussed this but could find not find any answers.

'They had not taken Asari. She was still very sick but I knew that, with hope in her heart, she would recover in a few days.

'Alik decided to take a risk. He could speak the white men's language, he had been taught by a white man in the school near his village. When our captors came with our meal that day, Alik spoke to one of them directly, 'Why did you kill the sick slaves?' he asked. 'For insurance,' the white man replied. He paused for a moment and then added, 'They would have died anyway. In any case, the sick will spread disease and everyone will die. We killed them to prevent you from getting sick.' He moved on with his bucket of rice. Neither of us understood the word 'insurance' so we were still mystified. Perhaps they felt that it was better to lose some of us than to risk losing all of us to disease.

'I was terrified. Would they be back again tomorrow to look for the sick? Alik and I spoke to Asari and told her that she had to sit up and look cheerful every time the white men came to the hold. I knew that if we made it to Jamaica, we would have a happy life together. Even if we were in chains, if Asari and I were together, we would have a beautiful life. Our love would make us happy. The white men must not discover that she was sick. I felt consumed by fear.

A Story Hidden in the Depths

'We returned to our corner of the hold and Alik began to speak to the others seated next to us. He tried to rouse them to revolt, to try to kill the white men if they came back again to take away the sick. But the slaves were afraid of the white men's guns. They would not risk getting shot when the sick would probably die anyway. Alik berated them for being weak and cowards but they turned their heads away.

'The white men returned the following day. Asari sat up smiling even though she was in terrible pain. They took more than forty people that day. Some resisted and were mercilessly beaten. We looked on in silence. Along with our freedom they had taken our anger from us and we tried not to listen to the terrible sounds from the deck.

'But I was happy that Asari was safe. I was happy even though people around me were dying. Alik said, 'We are cowards. We can kill the white man. We can trample him under our feet and crush his skull. There are so many of us!' but no one listened to him, they feared for their own lives. Even I turned away from this, from his anger. What if they shot me and Asari was left alone? I wanted to live for the beautiful life that waited for us in Jamaica. I wanted to live so that I could hold Asari in my arms and embrace her. I wanted to live to bring fish home every evening for Asari, so that we could lie together under the night sky and sing songs about the Niger River and our land in Africa. I did not want to die.

'When they returned again the next morning, Alik tried to get up, anger pulsing through him. I held him back and whispered that he must not fight against them alone, he would surely die. He sat down again, his body rigid.

'The white men continued their search for the sick. Asari sat up and smiled at me across the hold. I admired her courage but my heart pounded with fear. One of the white men glanced at her and then looked away. They took twenty-five that day. As they climbed up to the deck, Alik heard one of them say, 'This is the last batch. I think there are no more sick left.' When Alik translated what they had said, I slumped with relief. Asari was safe. I knew then that nothing could come between us and our dreams. As the white men pushed the sick slaves out of the hold, I said, 'They are gone.' I looked across at Asari and smiled.

'Suddenly, a loud voice shouted, 'SICK!' The white men turned at the top of the ladder to see where the voice came from. Chima shouted again, 'SICK!' He pointed at Asari. In that moment, my world collapsed.

'One of the white men climbed back down and walked over to Asari. He looked at her carefully. She closed her eyes. She knew that it was all over. I looked at Alik and he understood. We got up and moved towards the white man as he stood over Asari. I was shouting incoherently. But we had barely taken a few steps when I was hit hard on my head and lost consciousness.

'When I regained consciousness, I knew by the expression on Alik's face that it was all over. He looked away from me as he spoke, 'They took her. She is dead. As she left, she called out to me to take care of you and to tell you that this world is too small for your love.' I cried out at fate. The world had ended for me. My dreams were shattered. I was filled with rage and I lifted my face and looked at Alik. He understood and nodded.

'Together, we walked towards Chima. He looked at us and laughed and then he saw the fury in my eyes. He shrank away from me. I kicked him on his face and then Alik kicked him. He shrieked in pain and blood oozed from his nose. I felt no mercy. I kicked him again and again until his shrieks became whimpers. I kicked him until he was silent and only then we left.

'That night I could not sleep as I seethed with anger. This cruel ugly life had taken my mother, father and my home from me. And now it had taken Asari. I hated this world.

'The next morning life returned to some normality for the others. The massacre was over, there were no sick slaves left and there was more space for each of us. There was extra food. The white men came once more to take us to the deck for some fresh air. But my heart overflowed with anger. I wanted to kill everyone who had destroyed my dreams. What was the point? Asari would never come back and, with her, my dreams.

'I climbed on deck with the others as I used to before they took Asari, but the fresh air and the spray from the sea no longer revived me. A storm raged in my mind. I turned and stood before the slaves and told them we had to kill ourselves. Our guards stood looking out to sea, safe in the knowledge that they carried guns. We were no threat to them. I looked at the group of my fellow slaves who stood around me and repeated that we must kill ourselves to show the white men that though they controlled our lives, we controlled our deaths. I told them that life in Jamaica would not be any better. I spoke for a long time and told them that death is better than this life of wretched slavery. We had to show the white man that we would not bow to his will. We would choose our time and place of death. Alik looked steadily at me, his eyes bright.

'Alik closed his eyes as I stared out to sea. This was the ocean that lay between me and my beloved land, the same ocean that had taken Asari. I looked at the sea and thought about Asari and I spoke to her in my thoughts, 'Asari, I told you that I would give my life for you. That was my gift to win your heart. My life is the only thing that I now own. And that is the only gift that I can give you.' I looked at Alik. He smiled and I knew he understood.

"I hope that one day someone with a sensitive heart will hear our story,' I said to him. Alik nodded. 'Yes, one day a kind heart will learn our story from the sea,' he promised.

'And then, we ran. We ran towards the bow of the ship. Although we were tied together, we moved swiftly to embrace the sea. Something in the freedom of our running bodies seemed to shake the other slaves from their torpor and they began to run too. Too late, the white men realised what we meant to do and moved towards us but they were too far away. Alik shouted, 'Our brothers are coming with us.' I cried out, 'We have won.

A Story Hidden in the Depths

No one can make slaves of us anymore! Death is ours, not theirs. We die because we choose to!'

'Our hands and legs still tied together, we leapt into the sea.

'Alik had promised that someday someone travelling on this ocean would hear our story. Destiny has chosen you, for this is not just my story, it is your story too."

"Life is beautiful," said Jem's sad deep voice, "but only if you are free. I had love in my heart but slavery denied me the happiness that it would bring. Human love, bravery, ideals need freedom to bear fruit. Freedom is the ground on which life can be purposefully lived. Never chain a man's body or his mind because these bonds take away all that is meaningful in life. Freedom is the first ethic, from that are born higher ideals. Seek to be free and respect the freedom of others."

Mary's eyes flew open as the loud music and raised voices from the party on deck crashed in on her. The sad deep voice had gone. Something inside her had changed, been transformed. She left her cabin and walked to a secluded corner of the ship. She leant on the rail and stared out over the ocean. A perfect story waited to be written but that is not what made her happy. At some deep level, while she lay there listening to Jem's voice, she had understood the value of freedom. Her heart opened in gratitude, she thanked the sea for her wonderful story but also for the renewed sense of purpose she felt. She wanted to spread the message of freedom and liberty through her writing. She appreciated that her life was full of choices. Each day brought choices; what to eat, what to wear, where to go, what to do. She had taken for granted the luxury of having so much freedom in her world. Jem's tragic life had made her understand that many are denied even the most basic rights; they live and die in bondage. And all because a few men who hold power decide how others live and die.

Mary's family were delighted that the cruise had done her so much good. She smiled secretly when they commented on her calmness, putting it down to the company on board ship and the fresh ocean breeze.

Alone in her study, Mary sat lost in thought. Was the voice a figment of her imagination? Had she dreamt it? On an impulse, Mary searched for *Zong* on the internet. She gasped in shock as numerous listings appeared on the screen in front of her. The *Zong* was a real ship and the *Zong* massacre of 1781 a real event. One hundred and twenty two slaves had been killed between 29th November and 1st December of that year on the orders of the captain. He believed that he would be able to claim insurance for the slaves he had thrown overboard as their deaths would halt the spread of disease and thus prevent the loss of all his cargo. Ten slaves had jumped into the sea in an act of defiance against slavery. Mary felt her heart ache but she read on. There had been a fierce legal battle between the insurers and the company that owned the *Zong*. Mary felt sick as she realized that they were not being tried for murder but were haggling over whether insurance money was due for the slaves

A Story Hidden in the Depths

that had been killed. The human cargo was valued at 30 pounds sterling per head.

Months later, Mary's book had been written and published. It sold well and was translated into numerous languages. Its message of freedom resonated with its readers.

Mary was happy she had fulfilled Alik's promise. Jem's story, and that of all the others sold into slavery, was no longer a small incident in history but had become real to all her readers. The popularity of her book meant that it was written about and discussed, the story of the *Zong* had become common knowledge and would soon be made into a film: the shocking incident in which the captain of the *Zong* had ordered 122 slaves to be massacred for insurance money.

In the back of her mind, Mary still wondered where the voice had come from and why she had been chosen to hear it, but she had little time to ponder this as she travelled the world promoting her book. Seven months after her book was published, Mary was invited to London to appear on a television programme and to join in a debate on freedom. She decided to take the opportunity to spend time with her grandmother in Liverpool. She was seldom able to visit her and it had been six years since she had last seen her. Effie Gray was now 91 years old and still in excellent health and overjoyed to see her granddaughter.

Mary and Mrs. Gray settled down for a long chat to catch up on each other's lives. When the conversation drifted towards Mrs. Gray's childhood, Mary listened avidly; she had always wanted to know more about the British branch of her family. When Mrs. Gray saw how interested her granddaughter was in all she had to say, she mentioned that her own father, Mary's great grandfather, had, at one time, prepared a detailed family tree and that she would be happy to show it to Mary. She told Mary where to look for it; it was kept in a drawer in her grandmother's room. As Mary lifted out the old manuscript, she could not contain her curiosity and immediately opened the carefully preserved sheet of paper. She sat down on her grandmother's bed and looked with wonder at the branches of her family tree spread across the yellowing document. Mary was amazed to see the effort that her great grandfather had put into his research. He had done a thorough job; most of the entries also noted her ancestors' professions, place of residence and date of birth. This was particularly impressive as it had all been done in days before the internet.

Mary gazed at all the names arranged in chronological order, and felt reverence for the men and women who had created her. She was the outcome of all these names in front of her; some part of her had been part of them and now she carried forward their genes. Through these names Mary felt linked to her past. Her hands were trembling with the weight of her own history contained in this old, yellowed sheet of paper.

She settled down to read the entries more closely. She scanned the first few names beginning in the year 1622 but as her eyes raced through the list, they were

A Story Hidden in the Depths

involuntarily drawn to the middle of the page and she froze in disbelief at what she saw written there. The entry read: *Luke Collingwood, Resident of Liverpool. Born 1733. General surgeon and captain of the ship, Zong.*

The Conquest

March 1221, on the west bank of the mighty river Indus, close to the small village of Hund, is camped the greatest army that the world has ever seen. It is the force of the Mongol, Genghiz Khan. The last few days have witnessed a bitter and bloody battle between Genghiz's army and the last remnants of the forces of Khwarezmid, led by Jalal-ud-Din. Jalal-ud-Din's men have suffered the worst possible defeat and have been almost annihilated and Jalal-ud-Din escaped by crossing the Indus. Genghiz has thus completed his conquest of the huge Khwarezmia Empire.

After the victory, Genghiz decides to stay for a few days by the Indus, near the village of Hund, before embarking on another conquest.

On the far side of the river, are camped the armies of Iltutmish, the Slave emperor of Delhi and Genghiz's reputation as a great conqueror and a cruel warrior has undoubtedly reached him. He knows that Genghiz's army is invincible and that something must be done to prevent it from marching on the beautiful and prosper-

The Conquest

ous kingdom built by him and his dynasty. His strategy is to send a vast army to camp near the Indus, and to pray day and night to God for a miracle that Genghiz will decide to turn back without overthrowing the Slave Dynasty and occupying his land.

Genghiz stands on the banks of the river and looks across at the great country spread before his eyes; the land of silk and spices, of a thousand gods, of the most beautiful music and the sweetest lyrics, the land of holy waters and spiritual inhabitants. This is Hindustan, protected by the massive barricade created by the gods themselves, the Himalayas.

Genghiz has heard much about Hindustan; he had grown up listening to stories of magic, treasure, fairies and fakirs. This land had always fascinated him, and today he stood just a river's breadth away from it. It seems as though destiny itself is inviting him to cross it. He looks at this land of his dreams and a smile appears on his rugged and battle worn face. His trusted general, Subutai, approaches him.

Subutai: Exalted Khagan, under your guidance we have achieved a great victory. The entire Khwarezmia Empire is now yours. No other kingdom in history has been as large or as great as yours.

Genghiz: We have indeed achieved a great victory, Subutai. However, there remains much to be done. The greatest conquests are yet to be made.

He smiles and continues to gaze at the land beyond the Indus.

Subutai [*looks troubled*]: If I may take the liberty of asking the great Khan a question. Do you mean to cross the Indus to conquer the spiritual land of Hindustan? Even the great Alexander... [*he stops as he realizes the folly of speaking Alexander's name*].

Genghiz [*face flushes with rage*]: Alexander! Who was Alexander? A spoilt boy who conquered a few bits of land because they were ruled by even smaller boys who did not know that fighting battles is harder than playing marbles! You dare compare the mighty Genghiz Khan with that clown! If he were alive today, he would have been a foot soldier in my army! I could have your head chopped off for speaking thus! And then you can join your friend Alexander in the other realm and play marbles together while I conquer Hindustan and then the whole world!

Subutai [*bows low*]: I humbly apologize, O Khan of Khans. I realize the foolishness of my statement. I will never speak of that infant again.

Genghiz [*takes a deep breath to calm down*]: Hindustan must be conquered. That would be the crown of the great Mongol empire. That would show the dazzling greatness of the Mongols to students of history even a thousand years from now. Do not forget that I am the envoy on

The Conquest

earth of "The Eternal Blue Sky" sent to rule all people and I wield its infinite power. I am destined to conquer the world. There is no place for fear. We must act.

Subutai bows his head.

Genghiz continues to stare across the mighty Indus. Civilizations have come and gone, some conquerors and others conquered, and they have worshipped this river, or filled it with the blood of battle. Its glistening waters have flowed through the twists and turns of history on its journey to the sea, uncaring of the events of man. Human history is just a bubble in the mighty flow of time. The river is only humbled at its source by the mighty Himalayas and dwarfed at its end by the Arabian Sea. The events of man leave no impression on it.

Genghiz: The Slave Dynasty of Delhi does not deserve to rule this great land. In a few days time it will be humbled and the heavenly gates of Hindustan will open to the great Mongols. Then the golden era for both these great nations will begin. Imagine the trade that will take place between Persia, Hindustan, China and Mongolia when they are a part of the same empire. The Slave Dynasty does not know that great battles are not won by numbers. They are won by superior tactics and an iron will.

Genghiz draws his sword and it glitters in the glare of the sun. Genghiz seems happy with his dramatic pose and continues to stand like that for a few minutes.

Subutai: That is true, O Khan of Khans. The Slave Dynasty will be defeated in a matter of days and Hindustan will be ours. [*Suddenly serious*] There are several places where the Indus may be crossed. One of these is near the village of Hund. There are some others further north. I suggest we move about a third of our men north and have them cross the river there at night. The rest of the army will cross at daybreak near Hund. When the battle begins, the soldiers from the north will attack from the rear and take the army of Iltutmish by surprise. There will be a moonless night four days from now, ideal for our men to cross the river under the cover of darkness. But you know, O invincible Khagan, the enemy soldiers are probably so terrified of your name that they will flee as soon as you shout the battle cry of *Morindoo*.

Genghiz: You are a very useful man, Subutai, and very talented in the art of warfare.

Subutai: I am your humble servant and whatever I know, I have learnt from you.

Genghiz: We have four days to rest and prepare. I wish to visit the village of Hund to see what it is like. This is the first time that I will enter a village without having destroyed it first. Maybe I am mellowing with age [*laughs loudly*]. Fetch a few horses and men, and let's go to this village. For our meal, we will plunder a household and force the family to cook food for us [*laughs again*].

The Conquest

Subutai arranges for a few horses and men to accompany them. Genghiz and Subutai ride towards Hund.

The village is small and poor and they enter it as the sun sets on the distant horizon. Most of the inhabitants are farmers who work the fields that surround Hund. There is one small shop that trades goods for wheat, a tailor, and a family of potters. It is a sleepy hamlet that finds entertainment in gossip but its unexciting life is overcome, from time to time, by events that shape the course of history. Hund is strategically located close to one of the crossing points on the Indus favoured by invaders of Hindustan who come from the West. The villagers dread this but at the same time it brings excitement to their quiet existence. As each new wave of aggressors sets up camp on the banks of the Indus, the men of Hund place bets on how close they will get to Delhi and whether they will successfully conquer it. The bets on the fortunes of Genghiz Khan are split almost halfway between his plundering Delhi and returning, and his conquering Delhi and staying on there as the new emperor of Hindustan. No one believes he will turn away without attempting to conquer Hindustan, and no one believes he will lose to the armies of Iltutmish. Anyone betting on something as silly as that would invite the laughter of the whole village.

Genghiz and his men slowly make their way along the narrow stone paths that run between the small mud houses. Most of the inhabitants have barricaded themselves inside their homes. Curious to see the famous invader, they peep through little holes in doors and windows made specifically for this purpose by the village carpenter. The carpenter, needless to say, is in great demand whenever there is news of a new invader crossing the Khyber Pass.

Genghiz: It is a dead village, Subutai. There seems to be no one about. Do they sleep so early in Hindustan?

Subutai: It is only because they are terrified of you, O great Khan. They have locked themselves inside their houses and are probably trembling with fear.

Genghiz smiles. He has always been proud of the fact that the very mention of his name strikes terror in the hearts of men and kings alike.

Genghiz: Look, Subutai! In this village of cowards there is one brave man. That door over there is open and it is decorated as if to invite us in [*points to a door at the end of the stone path*].

Subutai: Yes, I see that! It must be someone with no knowledge of current affairs or someone who is brave enough to open the door to meet the great Khan of Khans.

The men on horseback reach the door. The door and the outer wall of the house are more colourful and decorative than the other houses in the village.

The Conquest

Two clay lamps, *diyas*, are placed on either side of the gate. The door is wide open. It appears that the resident of the house is expecting guests.

Genghiz and Subutai dismount and walk through the door and find themselves in a courtyard.

The soldiers remain outside to guard the horses.

The spiritual scent of incense fills the air. It is mixed with the aroma of something cooking on a mud stove at the far end of the courtyard. On the floor on one side of the stove are placed two decorated mats. On the mats are two brass plates and some brass bowls. It seems that the resident of the house is definitely expecting someone for dinner.

Genghiz: The idiot is expecting someone for dinner. I am hungry too. I will command the owner of this house to serve us food.

Subutai: It seems like a very calm and peaceful place. I feel good here. Let me find out who is inside.

A woman sings inside the house. Her voice is sweet and musical. She hears the two men enter.

Female voice [*in a tone that is perfectly balanced between tenderness and firmness*]: You are late. I have been expecting you for some time now. Wash your hands from that ewer over there and sit on your mats. I will soon serve dinner.

Genghiz and Subutai look at each other in surprise. Genghiz smiles. His smile suggests that he wants to use this as an opportunity for a bit of amusement. Even the cruellest barbarians have the right to a practical joke followed by a good laugh. Genghiz thinks that he will soon be eating dinner meant for someone else. But then Genghiz has never minded taking what was meant for someone else. Indeed, he has made a career of it.

Genghiz and Subutai sit down on the mats and grin at each other.

Just then a woman walks across the courtyard and stands in front of them. She is draped in a bright blue *sari*. Its veil covers her head and she has pulled it forward to cover her face so that it cannot be seen. She is tall and slender.

Woman [*folds her hands to greet her guests*]: *Namaskar*! I am so glad that you could come for dinner. This house has been blessed.

Genghiz and Subutai are surprised that they are being treated as guests.

Woman [*her voice stern*]: So, you did not even wash your hands, eh? One should never eat food without washing one's hands. Come, I will pour water for you.

Genghiz and Subutai decide to do as they are told. They know, of course, that soon they will tell the woman who they are and then fear will strike her. *Poor soul, living in ignorance*, they think, as they extend their hands and the woman pours water for them.

Woman: I will fetch a lamp and some food.

The woman goes back inside the house and returns to the courtyard with a lamp and places it in front of her guests. Next, she carries dishes full of hot food and a basket of flat Indian bread, *chapatis*. She begins serving the food to Genghiz and Subutai who seem to be enjoying the experience and the delicious meal which is simple but well prepared: pulses, curried vegetables and *chapatis,* along with raw onions. They gorge on it.

The woman then serves them *kheer*, an Indian rice pudding. The Mongols enjoy eating it and even ask for a second helping.

At the end of the meal, the woman sits on a small wooden stool in front of the two men.

Genghiz [*in a loud voice*]: Do you know who I am?

Woman: You are my guest.

Genghiz [*voice thunders at her silly answer*]: Psha! Do you know who I am and where I have come from and what I have come here to do?

Woman [*calmly*]: Does it matter?

Genghiz: Yes, it matters! It matters to me! It matters to the whole world. And it will matter to you as soon as you learn who I am. You ignorant fool! You have served us dinner meant for someone else and you do not even want to know who we are [*he slams his fist on the empty brass plate making a loud clatter*]!

Woman [*unruffled*]: You think that it matters when in fact it does not. But since you seem so insistent that I know who you are, let me tell you who you are. But first let me say that this dinner was not meant for anyone else. I knew that one of these days, you would come here with your trusted general. I wished to meet you yesterday and I even went to your camp, but nobody would let me in. They said that the great Khan of Khans was busy with important work. I had to meet you, so I decided that I would wait for you to come here. All you conquerors are of a curious nature. I knew that you would explore this village and that you would only find the door of one house open. I decided to wait. If you had not come today, you would have come tomorrow.

Subutai and Genghiz exchange surprised looks.

Woman: And now let me tell you who you are. And I will tell you that in two parts. First, I will tell you how the world sees you, and then I will tell you who you really are. The world sees a great conqueror. You were born near the Burkhan Khaldun mountain in Mongolia. Your father was killed when you were nine and you and your

The Conquest

mother were exiled. As a child, you lived a life of poverty and survived on wild fruits and small game. You became the head of a small tribe and then began uniting other Mongol tribes. Soon, you created a huge army and started fighting against the great kingdoms of the world. You tore through the Great Wall and conquered the whole of China. After a few more years, you conquered Korea. Then you moved westwards and conquered everything that you saw and considered worth conquering. Your empire extends from the edge of Europe to the east end of Asia. You have more territory under your control than all of the previous invaders put together. The Mongols call you the Khan of Khans or the great Khagan. You are indeed the greatest conqueror the world has ever seen or will ever see.

Subutai and Genghiz are completely baffled at the amount that this woman, living in a small village on the banks of Indus, knows. Before either of them can speak, the woman continues.

Woman: And now to the more interesting subject of who you really are. You are a man who does not know how to find happiness. You are trying to fill the void of your lonely and unhappy heart by conquering the world. In the dust, sweat and blood of the battlefield you seek to attain what you could have had simply by looking at a placid lake or a field of flowers. You could have achieved fame and glory by singing songs, writing poetry or building monuments. But no, that is not enough. In your quest for happiness, others are compelled to take up arms for you or against you. Your need for glory has bathed the world in blood and forced it to forget the children that cross the path of your troops. You are a silly little boy who has grown to adulthood with no understanding of how to gain happiness or glory without having to pillage, plunder and destroy.

Genghiz is shaken. His face is flushed with anger. Subutai is shocked at the fearless words that the woman has spoken. He is certain that the woman will be brutally killed by Genghiz.

Genghiz [*shouting*]: How dare you speak to me like this? I can cut your head off in a second and then you will never speak again.

Woman [*very calmly*]: Do you think that I do not know that you execute anyone who dares to speak even a word against you? And do you really think that I fear such a thing? Ha!

Genghiz has never met anyone as fearless as this woman and, for the first time in his life, he is nonplussed.

Genghiz [*regaining his composure*]: You are indeed a fearless woman. And I *will* cut off your head. But first remove your veil so that I can see who I am speaking to. And I wish to know your name before I kill you [*he

The Conquest

places his hand on the handle of his sword and draws it partially out of its sheath].

Woman: My name is Maya. And I will not remove my veil.

Genghiz: Ha! Why not? Perhaps you are worried that your ugliness will make us laugh. [*Commandingly*] Remove your veil now.

Maya: We are discussing politics and conquests. And I want to tell you why you must not conquer more land, particularly the land on the far side of the Indus. The veil is not significant; faces should not matter. Ideas are important.

Genghiz [*angrily*]: Remove your veil and after that we will talk about politics or whatever else you wish. In fact, there will not be much to discuss once your head is separated from your body! I and my trusted general are skilled at making decisions about what we should and should not do. Remove it!

Maya [*softly*]: First tell me O Khan of Khans, is a sheathed sword more dangerous or an unsheathed one?

Genghiz: Stupid woman! An unsheathed one, of course.

Maya: Then why do you want me to remove my veil?

Genghiz: I do not see what your veil has to do with a sword. Remove it now!

Maya: Yes. If you insist, I will do it. But remember that you have asked for this. And you are right, for in a few moments we will have nothing to discuss because a discussion takes place between equals.

Maya pulls aside the veil of her *sari* and reveals an extraordinarily beautiful face. A delicate nose set above crimson lips, her eyes are deep and reflect a remarkable intelligence. She has beauty that inspires poets. She has beauty that makes men kill or be killed.

Genghiz and Subutai are struck dumb. They both become intensely self-conscious. Genghiz loses his grip on the handle of his sword, a sword that he had held tightly moments earlier.

Maya: I wished to converse with you without showing my face. I wanted a discussion between two minds. But you asked me to reveal my face. I said that faces are not important, but that is not true. Unfortunately, in our world they often matter more than minds. The sword has been unsheathed and now there may not be much dialogue between us [*smiles, in complete control of the situation*].

Genghiz [*softly, unable to take his eyes off her face*]: I do not understand. What dialogue?

The Conquest

Subutai looks at Genghiz. He has never seen him so hesitant.

Maya: I wanted to talk to you about your campaign to cross the Indus and invade Hindustan.

Genghiz: Why should I discuss that with you? Hindustan has always been my dream. I will conquer it and start a new age in this magical land.

Maya: I wanted to convince you not to invade Hindustan with the argument that this would take you too far from the core of your empire in Central Asia and will thereby weaken the whole domain. And I wanted to argue that Hindustan is made up of a large number of small kingdoms and to bring them under your control will take up so much time and effort that, in your absence, your generals and unscrupulous relatives will divide up your Chinese and Central Asian realms leaving you with nothing there. And then you will be emperor of Hindustan alone. You must also realize that your newly acquired Khwaremizian Empire needs particular attention. You will have to appoint an able governor very soon or there is the possibility of a revolt by the cities of Otrar and Samarkhand. And if none of these arguments had persuaded you, I would have told you that war itself is futile and the only way to achieve everlasting glory is by creation and not by destruction.

Genghiz [*intrigued*]: You say that these would have been your arguments. Why do you not use them to convince me now?

Maya: Because it is not necessary.

Genghiz: Because you have realized their futility or because you understand that the force of nature, Genghiz Khan, cannot be stopped.

Maya [*laughs*]: None of these.

Subutai: This woman is very well informed about you and your conquests. Her reasoning about the political consequences of a lengthy campaign in India makes sense and should be considered. She is indeed an intelligent and knowledgeable woman. But, O great Khan of Khans, why do we continue to listen to her? Your generals and advisers will discuss all this at length when we plan the campaign tomorrow.

Genghiz [*trembling with anger*]: Subutai! You are crossing your limits. I decide who I wish to talk to. If you utter one more word while I and Maya discuss my India campaign, I will have your body cut into a thousand pieces and fed to the fishes of the Indus who will relish the Mongolian delicacy.

Subutai: I apologize, O Khan of Khans. I will remain silent.

The Conquest

Subutai shakes his head in bewilderment. He cannot understand why Genghiz continues to converse with this strange woman. Genghiz rarely discussed matters with anyone, let alone a woman and a stranger.
Maya tries to stop herself from laughing.

Genghiz: So, why do you no longer want to discuss my campaign? You have nothing to say now, is that why?

Maya [*with a degree of arrogance*]: Because I no longer think it is necessary.

Genghiz: Why?

Maya: Because you will not cross the Indus. I know.

Genghiz looks stunned. Subutai gasps; he cannot make sense of this conversation between Genghiz and Maya.

Maya: You will not cross the Indus because I request you not to cross the Indus [*she laughs*]. No, let me make a more accurate statement. You will not cross the Indus because I order you not to cross the Indus.

Genghiz [*shouts*]: What? You order me? No one in my life has ever ordered me to do anything.

Maya [*slowly, speaking each word clearly*]:
Yes...I...order...you.

Genghiz: Why do you think that I will listen to you?

Maya [*firmly*]: Not only will you listen, you will agree.

Genghiz: Why?

Maya: Because you have fallen in love with me.

This statement hits them like a meteor falling on a rice field. Genghiz's mouth falls open, he is speechless. Subutai's eyes widen in shock. A long silence ensues. Maya smiles. The light of the lamp falls on one side of her face, the light of the moon on the other, adding a magical dimension to her beauty. This external light mixes with her inner radiance on the canvas of her face creating a sublime effect. Her exquisite beauty, her composure, her brilliant mind, her charm, her confidence, and her speech, make her irresistible.

Genghiz [*attempting to regain some composure*]: How do you know that I have fallen in love with you? I know nothing of love. It is an emotion that is felt only by the weak.

Maya: Genghiz! Or maybe I should address you by your childhood name, Temujin. Temujin, do you know if you have conquered Xia or Bukhara?

The Conquest

Subutai cannot believe that Maya has called Genghiz by his childhood name and is still alive.

Genghiz: Nobody has called me Temujin for so many years now. You know a lot about me [*smiles*]. Yes, I know that Xia and Bukhara have been conquered because I am the conqueror!

Maya: Precisely. You have the answer [*smiles*].

Genghiz: How so?

Maya: I know that you love me because I am the conqueror. A conqueror knows what he has conquered. And you said that love is an emotion felt only by the weak. That is not true. Love can make you weak. But then remember, love can also make you very strong. Yesterday you did not have love and were weak. Today you have fallen in love and have become strong.

Genghiz: Yesterday I was not weak. And I am the same today. In fact, I am the same every day.

Maya: Yesterday you were weak because you only thought about killing, looting and plundering for your own gain. But today is different. Today you have fallen in love. Today you will be able to do something that you could not do yesterday.

Genghiz: What?

Maya: Today you will give up a kingdom for someone else.

Genghiz remains silent, utterly amazed by this strange woman.

Maya: Today you will give up Hindustan for me. Today you will give up your dream just to win a smile on my face and some warmth in my heart for you.

Genghiz [*voice low as if he is in a trance*]: And you will smile if I do this? [*Suddenly shakes himself as if out of a dream and his voice becomes powerful again*] I have many wives. I have never fallen in love with any of them. What makes you think that I am in love with you?

Maya [*like a teacher explaining something to a pupil*]: Temujin, Temujin, Temujin, love is not about acquiring someone. Love is not something that you can buy or barter. Love is about giving yourself up for something as small as the smile on your loved one's face. You have never loved before because you have never met a woman who has stirred your soul. Your wives came to you because they had to; you took them from their homes or traded marriage for land. You could never love them because they submitted to your will. I do not submit to your will! I question all that you stand for. That makes you honour me. This is the first time in your life that you have given a woman respect. You look up to me because

The Conquest

I have challenged the way you think and because I have understood the depths of your heart. That is why you love me.

Genghiz [*very seriously*]: It is true that I have never given any woman respect. Today, when I met you, I thought that you were just one of countless women that look up to me. But I was wrong. You are beautiful but some of my slave girls are as beautiful as you. Yet, I do not love them. I feel nothing for them. They do not look at me with eyes that search my soul for its deepest meaning. They have become objects that I own. But you are different. There is magic about you. I feel trapped and I do not even want to get out [*these words seem to be drawn from him against his will*].

Maya: That is love. You have searched the world for something to fill the void in your heart. You can rule the world as its greatest emperor but it will not be enough. You need to conquer another's heart. And more, you need to be conquered yourself...by a woman. What you have always needed is love.

Genghiz: I will make you my queen and we will rule my great empire together.

Maya [*smiles*]: Temujin, remember that when you love someone, you should not impose your will on her. You should ask her what she wants.

Genghiz [*smitten*]: What do you want, my queen? I can place the world at your feet.

Maya: I want only two things: first, that you do not cross the Indus and second, that I will never be your queen.

Genghiz [*feeling betrayed*]: Why will you not be my queen? I love you. You yourself have told me that.

Maya: Yes, I told you that you love me. But I do not love you. I cannot be your queen because I do not love you. I did not want you to fall in love with me. That is why I came before you veiled. I wanted to try to convince you with logic, through discussion. You did not permit me to do that. You demanded I remove my veil and after that there was no longer any need of argument. You were conquered. Just as you are confident that you can cross the Indus to Hindustan and conquer it, so I was confident that I could conquer you at the first sight of my face.

Genghiz: No Hindustan, no Maya? What is in it for me?

Maya [*her voice soft and warm*]: Every evening at sunset, for the rest of my life, I will think about you and I will thank you for what you have done for me. I will look at the setting sun and say, "Thank you from the bottom of my heart for what you have done for me, *my* conqueror." [*Maya stresses the word* my].

The Conquest

Subutai shakes his head violently but Genghiz's eyes are fixed on Maya's luminous face.

Genghiz: It seems such an insignificant thing you offer me. Yet it seems like the greatest possession that I will ever have. If anyone had told me that I would give up even a small plot of land for a woman, let alone a great realm, I would have thought him insane. Today you ask me to give up Hindustan in return for nothing more than your smile and gratitude at every sunset and it seems enough. And you will call me *your* conqueror. [*He looks thoughtful*] How do I know that you will keep your word?

Maya: I promise you this by the waters that flow in the River Indus. For you conquerors, this river is the threshold of Hindustan, the place where the battle for this beautiful country begins. But this is also where countless love stories have blossomed and the river has blessed them all. I cannot lie when I swear by this river. I will do as I have promised. Every day, till I die!

Genghiz: I trust you. Completely. [*In a sentimental tone common to lovers though the ages*] I will trust you till the end of my....

Subutai realizes he has remained silent too long. He interrupts.

Subutai: O great Khan of Khans, first ask her who she is. I hope that she is not an emissary of the Slave king, Iltutmish.

Genghiz [*suddenly awakes from dreams of everlasting love and asks in a serious tone*]: Why do you ask me not to conquer Hindustan? Why is it so important to you? Have you been sent by Iltutmish to defeat me without a single drop of blood being shed?

Maya: No. I have come to you on my own. I do not know Iltutmish.

Genghiz: Then why? Why do you not want me to conquer Hindustan?

Maya [*a tear flows down her cheek. The light of the lamp makes it sparkle like a diamond*]: I am here because I am soon to be married to Gopal. I love him dearly and he loves me. He lives in a village on the far side of the Indus. The armies of Iltutmish came to his village and recruited him as a foot soldier to fight against you. Iltutmish plans to send the local village men against you to take some of the sting off your charging cavalry. Gopal will surely die on the battlefield. I beg you, do not cross the Indus. Please, save Gopal. Please, I beg you [*weeps bitterly*].

Genghiz [*heartbroken*]: You are leaving the emperor of the world for an ordinary village boy who cannot even make a proper foot soldier. Even that silly kid Alexander was better.

Maya: Love knows no logic. Just as you have never fallen in love with the daughter of a wealthy and powerful ruler, so I do not love a king. I love Gopal. You may be the emperor of the world but he is the emperor of my heart. If he dies, I will drown myself in the Indus so that we can meet again in heaven. I beg you to grant us life and to grant us love [*she folds her hands in supplication*].

Genghiz [*bows down to her and kisses her hand*]: I promise you, Maya, that I will not set foot across the Indus. I will begin my journey back to Central Asia tomorrow. Each morning, when the sun rises, I will pray that you and your love live a long and happy life together.

Maya: Thank you, my conqueror.

The next morning Maya goes to meet Genghiz at his camp.
    Genghiz's army has been ordered to march back to Central Asia. Genghiz sits on his horse and looks at the army of Iltutmish camped across the Indus. Subutai is by his side. Genghiz's face breaks into a smile when he sees Maya approaching them.

Maya [*offering him a piece of silk cloth*]: This is for you, Temujin. I have embroidered it in Hindi with the words, "Thank you, my conqueror." Keep it with you always and

I will keep my promise and utter these words everyday at sunset.

Genghiz kisses the cloth and waves goodbye to Maya, his eyes moist. Maya's eyes, too, are full of tears. Genghiz rides a short distance away and turns to Subutai.

Genghiz: She called me "*My* conqueror".

Subutai: You should never have asked her to remove the veil.

Genghiz [*angrily*]: Who are you to tell me what I should and should not do? I can do as I please. I can even cut your body into two parts and have one thrown here and one in Mongolia. That way your ghost will not know which land to haunt.

Subutai shakes his head.

Across the river, the forces of Iltutmish rejoice, proud that the mighty Genghiz Khan did not dare to cross the Indus. *The size of my army has repelled the greatest conqueror ever, and that too without a drop of blood being spilt,* thinks Iltutmish.

The villagers of Hund have all lost their bets. They decide to pool their losses and use them for the common good of the village.

Maya sits in her house with the door open waiting for someone to return. There are two *diyas* placed

The Conquest

outside the door. She makes *kheer* for the long awaited guest. As she stirs the pot, she smiles.

The Mongol Empire of Genghiz Khan was the largest contiguous empire in history. At its peak, it stretched from Eastern Europe to the Sea of Japan, nearly 10,000 kilometres across!

In 1221, Genghiz Khan and his general Subutai defeated the last remnants of the Khwarezmid Empire on the banks of the River Indus near the village of Hund and thus conquered nearly the whole of Asia. Fearing that Genghiz would invade India, Iltutmish, the Slave Emperor of Delhi, sent a huge army to confront him.

Genghiz Khan never crossed the Indus but turned his army away and marched back to Central Asia. Why he never attempted to conquer Hindustan is open to conjecture and is one of the enduring mysteries of history.

No More a Roving

On the 6th of July 1822, in a small room in the Italian port town of Livorno, Edward Ellerker Williams, a retired British naval officer, was writing to his wife, Jane Williams, who was staying at Villa Magni at Lerici. He wrote with great enthusiasm; he was eager to meet her and speak to her in person rather than having to write her a letter. Before sealing the letter in an envelope, he read it aloud to himself:

"I have just left the quay, my dearest girl, and the wind blows right across to Spezzia, which adds to the vexation I feel at being unable to leave this place. For my own part, I should have been with you in all probability on Wednesday evening, but I have been kept day after day, waiting for Shelley's definitive arrangements with Lord B. relative to poor Hunt, whom, in my opinion, he has treated vilely. A letter from Mary, of the most gloomy kind, reached S. yesterday, and this mood of hers aggravated my uneasiness to see you; for I am proud, dear girl, beyond words to express, in the

conviction, that wherever we may be together you could be cheerful and contented.

Would I could take the present gale by the wings and reach you to-night; hard as it blows, I would venture across for such a reward.[1]"

On the 8th of July 1822, Edward Williams and Percy Bysshe Shelley, along with a boat boy, were aboard a schooner out at sea. About an hour had passed since they set sail from Livorno and they were making their way steadily towards Lerici. It had been calm when they set sail but in about a quarter of an hour, the seas had become choppy. The boat boy managed the craft alone, leaving Williams and Shelley free to gaze at the beautiful Mediterranean Sea.

"I felt that poor Hunt was treated most unfairly by Lord Byron," said Williams. "I observed dejection in his manner and voice when Lord Byron expressed little interest in creating the journal."

Shelley nodded, "I could not agree more. Poor Hunt! He deserved better. I am put out with Byron myself."

Shelley and Byron had come up with a plan to publish a new journal. *The Liberal* was to be the voice of the free-thinking individual and a counter to the conservative *The Quarterly Review*. Leigh Hunt, an editor and himself a poet, had not been doing too well in England and on Shelley's insistence, Hunt left England to join him in Italy.

---

[1] This letter was actually written by Edward Williams

"We were keen on Hunt joining us as editor," Shelley said, "it all seemed perfect and Byron, at one time, appeared even keener than I was to have Hunt join us and to begin writing the journal at once. Hunt is a fine gentleman. He came to Italy because of us but he got here only to find that Byron had changed his mind and was now opposed to the idea of the journal. Why did he not consider the matter carefully before he agreed to invite Hunt? I am quite incensed with Byron. He seems to think that he can get away with anything. Not this time. Not this time! I will see to it that the journal is published, Byron or no Byron."

Shelley was thoughtful for a moment before he continued, "I must say, though, that this venture will be far harder without Byron's wealth, support and contacts in the Italian publishing world."

"Lord Byron can indeed be difficult," said Williams.

"Difficult? Impossible!" the words burst forth from Shelley. "When Mary and I bought this boat, we argued for days on what to name it. Before we had a chance to make up our minds, Trelawny named it *Don Juan*. Mary was quite vexed at this announcement by him. I do understand how she felt. It is my schooner so why should it be named for a poem by Byron? The following day, Mary and I decided to name it *Ariel*. It was Ariel, as you well know, who caused the storm in Shakespeare's *The Tempest*. We were both happy with the name and were preparing to have it painted on the mast. Before this could be accomplished, Lord Byron had *Don Juan* painted on the sail. Byron wishes the title of *his* poem to be painted on *my* ship. Difficult, you say? No Sir! He is impossible!"

"He is really a most unconventional character," Williams said. "He seems a different person each time I meet him. Sometimes he is full of charm, and makes those around him feel special, but at others he is irritable and rude. Sometimes he appears to be a genius with an extraordinary memory and intellect but then he can appear to be mentally ill and melancholic. I am not able to understand him at all."

"It is not possible to understand him," Shelley said firmly. "You can love him, or you can hate him but you cannot understand him. Many of us, and I include myself in this, love and hate him at the same time. I am often annoyed by him but I cannot overlook the immense influence he has had upon me and upon my poetry. Had I not spent hours in conversation and debate with Lord Byron while sailing on Lake Geneva, I could not have written "Hymn to Intellectual Beauty"."

Williams looked doubtful, "Perhaps he may inspire some poets to write but he causes the death of others by savage criticism."

"I know to whom you refer," Shelley nodded. "It is indeed commonly believed that Byron's criticism caused Keats to slide into a world of depression and that, coupled with consumption, killed him. It is tragic that poor John died at such a young age. But on this point I must disagree. While Byron could, perhaps, have been kinder in his criticism, he is as much entitled to his opinion as any one of us."

After considering for a moment, Shelley continued, "I think that Keats disliked Byron more than Byron did Keats. Think about it from Keats' point of view. He was a poor and struggling poet who found it difficult to have his poems published and read. Byron is a handsome, witty, flamboyant nobleman with easy access to the elite social classes of England. His poems are widely appreciated. Beset by failure, it is perhaps natural to be jealous of those who achieve success without much struggle. Keats found it unfair that he had to suffer for his art whereas Byron never had to struggle. I learnt that Keats, on hearing of a favourable review of Byron's work, once remarked to a friend, 'You see what it is to be six foot tall and a lord!' Keats' dislike of Byron and his poetry is coloured by envy but Byron's criticism of Keats, I feel, is informed by poetic aesthetics. I do not think that Byron understood the sensitivity to criticism of a poet like Keats and how it was the cause of his depression and death. Let me quote Canto XI from "Don Juan":

> 'John Keats, who was killed off by one critique,
> Just as he really promised something great,
> If not intelligible, - without Greek
> Contrived to talk about the Gods of late,
> Much as they might have been supposed to speak.
> Poor fellow! His was an untoward fate: -
> 'Tis strange the mind, that very fiery particle,
> Should let itself be snuffed out by an Article."

"It is indeed sad that Keats died at such a young age," Williams said, "but let me ask you, what did *you* think of his poetry?"

"I thought very highly of him as a poet," Shelley replied, "though I advised him on more than one occasion not to publish his early works. I liked him as a person too, though I agree with Byron that he was an oversensitive fellow. He often took exception to my advice. I have always believed that his poetry will be recognised one day. Byron disagrees and disapproves of my support for Keats but then Byron is Byron. When Keats was ill and wished to travel to Italy, I invited him to stay with us but he did not come. Inspired by his death, about a year ago I wrote "Adonais":

> 'I weep for Adonais - he is dead!
> Oh, weep for Adonais! though our tears
> Thaw not the frost which binds so dear a head!
> And thou, sad Hour, selected from all years
> To mourn our loss, rouse thy obscure compeers,
> And teach them thine own sorrow, say: With me
> Died Adonais; till the Future dares
> Forget the Past, his fate and fame shall be
> An echo and a light unto eternity!"

"It is a long poem and these are the last four lines," Shelley continued to recite from "Adonais":

> "I am borne darkly, fearfully, afar;
> Whilst, burning through the inmost veil of Heaven,

The soul of Adonais, like a star,
Beacons from the abode where the Eternal are."

Williams was moved, "That is beautiful poetry."

"I am still not happy with it. I think that it has much room for improvement. I consider it my most imperfect work."

The wind had strengthened and the sea had grown rougher. However, the boat boy was skillful and had no difficulty in controlling the vessel. Shelley and Williams were silent as they looked out over the storm tossed Mediterranean.

Suddenly Shelley asked, "Where did you and Jane meet?"

"In India, actually," replied Williams, "Jane's brother is a general in the army in Madras. She was married when she was sixteen to a naval captain in the East India Company but he was a despicable fellow. She went through torment before we met and fell in love. With the support of her brother, she separated from him and now we are together. That little girl deserves all the happiness life has to offer. She had always yearned to see Europe, and particularly Italy, and that is why we came here to live. The fact that rents in the charming town of Lerici are a fraction of what we would have had to pay in England is a bonus."

Both men were silent again, deep in thought. After some moments, Williams turned purposefully towards Shelley and said, "There is something I have wanted to ask you for a long time. I apologise for being so direct but this question has troubled me and must be asked."

"What is it Edward? You are a good friend. Do not hesitate, if I can put your mind at ease."

"Do you love Jane?"

"What?" Shelley was taken aback; he had not been expecting this.

"Shelley, do you love my wife?"

"That is a very difficult question to answer. Not because the answer is difficult but because the answer may be difficult for you to understand. The answer will depend on how you define love, a word that is used in so many different ways that I have grown weary of its usage. I once wrote:

> 'One word is too often profaned
> For me to profane it,
> One feeling too falsely disdain'd
> For thee to disdain it.
> One hope....."

Shelley stopped abruptly in the middle of his recitation.

"Go on Shelley. Why did you stop? Go on."

Shelley began again and his voice grew stronger as he recited:

> "One word is too often profaned
> For me to profane it,
> One feeling too falsely disdain'd
> For thee to disdain it.

Shadows of Lost Time

One hope is too like despair
For prudence to smother,
And pity from thee more dear
Than that from another.

'I can give not what men call love;
But wilt thou accept not
The worship the heart lifts above
And the Heavens reject not:
The desire of the moth for the star,
Of the night for the morrow,
The devotion to something afar
 From the sphere of our sorrow?"

"Did you write this for Jane?"
 "Yes, I did."
 "Then you do love her."
 "I ask you again, how do you define the word love? I have heard it used in so many different ways that I no longer know in what context to use it."
 "I use the word in the sense of the love a man feels for a woman."
 "Then I ask you, is there only one kind of love between a man and a woman?"
 "Would your fondness for Jane have been different had she not been a woman?"
 "Would a son's love for his mother have been different had she been his father instead? Would a brother's love for his sister change if she had been his

brother? Of course! Of course! Of course!" Shelley sounded exasperated.

"Can you answer a simple question? Do you love my wife?" Williams was beginning to sound annoyed.

"Yes, I do, but not in the way you may think," Shelley replied, "I love her in the purest sense of the word. I love her in a way that is detached from what she feels for me. I love her in a way that makes me feel happy when I see her happy with you."

Williams' voice shook with anger, "I trusted you as a friend and you..." he hesitated as he groped for words, "all you poets are alike. All you poets!"

"Do all naval officers have the same code of ethics? Were the morals of the officer who married Jane the same as yours? Do you also abuse her the way he did?" Shelley was angry too.

"No! I am not like him," Williams was insulted, "he and I are very different!"

"Then why do you think that we poets are all the same?" Shelley took a deep breath and felt calmer. "How many poets do you know? You know Lord Byron and you know me and you think that qualifies you to pass judgments on all poets!"

"Lord Byron has no morals at all. I have told Jane to stay away from him."

"You did?" Shelley laughed. "I fear *you* would never be able to comprehend Byron's moral code. I wonder, does he even have one? Perhaps it can be expressed in a single word. Hedonism! He certainly has a strange power over women. They are drawn to him like moths to a flame. Maybe it is his looks, or his wealth, his poetry, his position, or his reputation of being dangerous. It is probably a combination of all these. Lord Byron is aware of his power and uses it to his full advantage. In a certain sense, "Don Juan" is an autobiography:

> 'Few things surpass old wine; and they may preach
> Who please, the more because they preach in vain.
> Let us have wine and women, mirth and laughter,
> Sermons and soda water the day after."

Then Shelley asked, "Do you know why Lord Byron is on self imposed exile?"

"He told me that he had removed himself from the stifling attitude of the English public because it adversely affected his work and poetry. He also told me that by traveling through Europe he hopes to gain a wider perspective on life," Williams ventured.

"Ha! He tells that to everyone," Shelley was scornful. "Actually, his numerous scandalous affairs, allegations of homosexuality, and the incestuous affair with his half-sister, Augusta Leigh, compelled him to run away. The fact is that if he were still in England and the charges proved, he would have been imprisoned and disgraced."

"God! These poets!" Williams was shocked.

"I am offended by your repeated reference to what you think is the normal behaviour of poets. My code of conduct is not the same as Byron's. We are the best of friends because of our common love of poetry and a belief in the right to freedom of speech. Our ideals on love and morality, however, are poles apart."

"And if I may be so bold, what are your ideals?" asked Williams.

Shelley seemed happy to respond, "You might as well go to a gin shop for a leg of mutton as expect anything human or earthly from me. I am a believer in non-violent struggle and free speech. I care little for fame. Are you aware that no more than fifty people have read my works and forty pounds is all that I have earned from publishing them. Yet I write. I do not write for money or fame but because I must; I have an unbearable urge to do so. I have no belief in God but an unshakable belief in the heights that the mind of man can reach. I was rusticated from Oxford for my pamphlet *The Necessity of Atheism*. I do not believe, as Wordsworth did, that beauty is a characteristic of objects around us. Like Plato, I believe that beauty is within our minds and that is where it must be sought. Let me quote to you from my "Hymn to Intellectual Beauty":

> 'Thus let thy power, which like the truth
> Of nature on my passive youth
> Descended, to my onward life supply
> Its calm - to one who worships thee,
> And every form containing thee,
> Whom, Spirit fair, thy spells did bind
> To fear himself, and love all human kind.

'And just as I believe in an ideal and abstract beauty that is not tied to physical objects, similarly I believe in ideal love of the kind that Plato espoused," Shelley continued. "Ideal love is not merely physical or bound to one person. It is a property of the mind and mind alone. And then, when one believes in Ideal love, why should it be restricted to one of the countless beautiful souls that exist around us. I express this in "Epipsychidion":

> 'Thy wisdom speaks in me, and bids me dare
> Beacon the rocks on which high hearts are wrecked.
> I never was attached to that great sect,
> Whose doctrine is, that each one should select
> Out of the crowd a mistress or a friend,
> And all the rest, though fair and wise, commend
> To cold oblivion, though it is in the code
> Of modern morals, and the beaten road.

'And it is love that takes us to a higher plane which some call God. Love and worship are one."

Williams was awed by the philosophy and sublime flight of ideals that Shelley expressed in his poetry. He was happy when Shelley continued to quote from "Epipsychidion":

> "What have I dared? Where am I lifted? How
> Shall I descend, and perish not? I know
> That Love makes all things equal: I have heard
> By mine own heart this joyous truth averred:

The spirit of the worm beneath the sod
In love and worship, blends itself with God."

Finally Shelley said, "Yes, I love Jane but in a way that is spiritual and abstract. I have not a particle of jealousy of her infinite love for you. I love in a way that elevates my mind and heart to the level of worship. It is a love that I am proud of and it is a love that need not worry you. If you still think that I have sinned or caused you harm, then you are free to punish me in whatever way you think appropriate."

Williams was relieved and felt ashamed of his suspicion, "I have doubted you, my friend, and for that I am sorry. Your understanding of love is very different from the sense in which it is used by most people in this world. You are right, I am mistaken. It is hatred that must be despised, not love, which is the purest and greatest of all human emotions. I feel ashamed that my love for Jane led me to jealousy and doubt and, ultimately, to hatred."

The sea had become very rough and the waves threatened to topple the vessel. The boat boy was doing a fine job and Williams, himself a master at sailing, was not unduly worried and continued their conversation.

"I was so overpowered by my doubts about your feelings for Jane, and so jealous of Jane's admiration for your poetry, that I embarked on this journey for only one reason: to kill you. I had planned to push you overboard and later to explain to the world that you had been swept into the sea during the storm. You see, I knew that a storm was forecast and that it would be upon us as we sailed. You will recall that I postponed our departure by one day. It was for this reason; so that we would be at sea on the day that the storm was expected. Now, I am sorry. The storm was really in my heart and mind. I am ashamed. My lovely Jane, how will I face her with this shame in my heart?" Williams covered his face with his hands, overcome by remorse.

"So you planned to kill me?" surprisingly, Shelley smiled. "I find that quite amusing. We will never tell Jane about our conversation. What we spoke of on this voyage will only be known by the two of us."

"I am grateful to you, Shelley. And please forgive the madness that overpowered me with such evil passion."

"Are you afraid of death, Edward?"

"Yes, I am. I wish to live for the love that I have for Jane and the love that she has for me. And you, Shelley?"

"I have no love for life. It is merely a painted veil that obscures the immortal spirit. In the battle between the immortal spirit and mortal life, it is life that wins. That is the greatest tragedy! Our love for life and its mundane needs and desires kills our love for the ideals of the spirit. Only two men have achieved the triumph of the spirit over life, Socrates and Jesus. Their spirits remained uncrushed by the societies of their age. And they gave up their lives for their spiritual beliefs. The rest of us live in the bleak and tragic triumph of life.

'The illusion of life, though inferior, destroys the spirit and curbs its sublime nature. Only love can help the spirit triumph over the mirage of life. I am writing a poem "The Triumph of Life":

> 'All but the sacred few who could not tame
> Their spirits to the Conqueror, but as soon
> As they had touched the world with living flame
> Fled back like eagles to their native noon.
>
> 'Of him whom from the lowest depths of hell
> Through every Paradise and through all glory
> Love led serene, and who returned to tell
> In words of hate and awe—the wondrous story
> How all things are transfigured except Love"

The storm grew steadily fiercer and the wind picked up speed. The men had to shout in order to be audible to each other.

"This storm can give us quite a lot of trouble," Williams was worried.

"Do you mean that we will drown?" Shelley was calm though he had to shout to be heard.

"No, I do not. Do not be so pessimistic. I have faced rougher weather in my life. However, we may be blown off course, that is all. It means that I will not meet Jane for yet another day. Poor girl, she will be so worried. And poor Mary, she will be worried too."

"I do not care if we live or die. I know that I will die soon. If not in this storm then soon afterwards," Shelley was matter of fact.

"Why do you say that?" Williams was shocked. "Don't talk about death in that way. We have to live. I have to live. I must live for Jane."

"I know that I will die soon because I have seen my doppelganger. And when death comes, I will welcome her with open arms. Let the illusion of life be over. I want to exist as a pure and immortal spirit."

"Doppelganger? What? Do you believe these things? I think it is your imagination, my friend."

"No, my dear Edward. I have met that creature. Jane has seen him, too. I shall welcome death. Let it come. I am disillusioned with life:

> 'All things that we love and cherish,
> Like ourselves, must fade and perish
> Such is our rude mortal lot,
> Love itself would, did they not."

Williams moved away to join the boat boy to assist him in piloting the vessel. The rain was torrential and the boat was tossed about wildly on the roiling sea. Shelley continued to stand calmly amidst the raging storm around him.

Suddenly, there was the deafening sound of tearing wood.

Five weeks later, on the 15th of August 1822, three men, Byron, Trelawny and Hunt, were on the beach near Viareggio. They stood near a burning pyre. A short distance away another pyre burned. Byron was uncharacteristically quiet as he stared into the flames.

Half a mile distant from the pyres, a carriage waited. Seated within it were two women, Jane Williams and Mary Shelley. Jane was inconsolable. Mary's face was expressionless as she looked at the fires burning in the distance.

Back on the beach, Trelawny spoke, "Death is cruel. They were two great men."

"He will never be with us again," Lord Byron said, almost to himself:

> "So we'll go no more a-roving
> So late into the night,
> Though the heart be still as loving,
> And the moon be still as bright.
>
> For the sword outwears its sheath,
> And the soul wears out the breast,
> And the heart must pause to breathe,
> And love itself have rest."

When the fire was reduced to ashes, Trelawny searched among them for the bones of Shelley. They had been consumed by the flames but a few charred pieces remained. Amongst them, Trelawny was astonished to find Shelley's heart, still intact. He picked it up and walked towards Mary Shelley and placed it in her hand. Mary held it up high and wept.

It had been a grey day followed by a gloomy dusk. The sky was overcast and the sea dark, as if reflecting the melancholy of the death of Shelley and his friend Williams. Hunt looked up at the moon and softly recited Shelly's poem:

> "Art thou pale for weariness?
> Of climbing heaven and gazing on the earth,
> Wandering companionless
> Among the stars that have a different birth, -
> And ever changing, like a joyless eye
> That finds no object worth its constancy?"

On the 16th of August 1822, the sun had set on Lord Byron's villa in Lerici. In a luxurious room ablaze with candles, Lord Byron and Jane Williams were seated facing each other.

Lord Byron's fingers traced the outlines of Jane's cheeks and lips:

> "Here, I can trace the locks of gold
> Which round thy snowy forehead wave;
> The cheeks which sprung from Beauty's mould,
> The lips, which made me Beauty's slave."

"Gordon. My beloved, Lord Byron!" Jane breathed.
"My lovely Jane."
"We are together. At last, there is nobody between us. I can scarcely believe that this has happened."

No More a Roving

"It happed for love, my dear! For love! For pure uninterrupted, undisturbed love:

> 'There is a Form on which these eyes
> Have fondly gazed with such delight--
> By day, that Form their joy supplies,
> And Dreams restore it, through the night.
>
> 'There is a Face whose Blushes tell
> Affection's tale upon the cheek,
> But pallid at our fond farewell,
> Proclaims more love than words can speak.
>
> 'There is a Lip, which mine has prest,
> But none had ever prest before;
> It vowed to make me sweetly blest,
> That mine alone should press it more."

Byron gazed into Jane's eyes as he recited his poem but momentarily his thoughts were turned away from her.

Like Williams, Byron, too, had known that there would be a storm that fateful night. Now, no one would ever know of the fishing vessel that had deliberately rammed into the *Ariel* as it tossed about on the churning sea. Byron hid a triumphant smile as he said to himself: *No, not the* Ariel. *I mean, of course, the* Don Juan.

Shelley, Keats and Byron were 19th century romantic poets and were closely associated with each other.

Shelley drowned under mysterious circumstances while sailing from Livorno to Lerici on board his schooner, the Don Juan. *The date was 8th July 1822, one month before his 30th birthday.*

The personalities and events in this story are based on historical research. The conversation on board Don Juan *is an imagined one. The role of Byron and Jane Williams in the death of Shelley is fiction.*

Renaissance

Maria could barely control her excitement. It was her birthday; but that was not the cause of it. Her father had promised her that he would take Maria, her sister Teresa, and their mother, Anna Fortunata, to visit Rome and the Vatican and she had been looking forward to the trip for more than a month now.

Maria's father, Pietro Agnesi, had made his fortune as a silk merchant. For him, wealth was not an end in itself but a means to maintain his social status, and he valued the society of the intellectual elite over the merely rich and fashionable. He would invite poets, musicians, painters, mathematicians and philosophers from Milan and the University of Bologna to his academic evenings which he held regularly.

Pietro wanted his daughters to have the best possible education so that they would be equipped to live the life of cultured noblewomen of the Milanese elite. And to this end, he wished to expose them to the beautiful art and architecture of the age in which they lived. Maria's eighth birthday was on the 16th of May in the year 1726:

she was a child of the Renaissance era, a period of renewed interest in the art, culture and philosophy of the ancient Greeks. The dark ages had passed and the love for knowledge and art that was central to classical antiquity had been reborn.

"Tomorrow we will see works by some of the greatest painters of the Renaissance era," Maria's father sounded enthusiastic but he was secretly worried that the sightseeing trip would not interest Maria and Teresa for whom the greatest delight was playing in the garden of their villa in Milan. Pietro Agnesi was about to discover what an extraordinary little girl Maria was.

The highlight of their first day of sightseeing was the greatest living symbol of ancient Roman architecture, the Colosseum. The massive amphitheatre was built to seat more than 45,000 spectators who came to watch gladiators in combat with wild beasts of all kinds, including lions, elephants and hyenas. Maria and Teresa were horrified to learn that during the inaugural games in 80 AD that lasted for 100 days, more than 2000 gladiators and 5000 animals had been killed.

The following morning the family visited the Sistine Chapel in the Vatican City. Pietro told them that its architecture had been inspired by the Temple of Solomon in the Old Testament. Maria stood amazed as she stared up at the massive fresco painted on the ceiling of the chapel and questions poured from her. She wanted to know how Michelangelo had been able to climb up and paint the ceiling. How long had it taken him? Pietro was an educated man but he was beginning to find his knowledge inadequate before the dazzling curiosity of Maria.

"Why is God reaching out his hand to touch Adam, father?" and before Pietro could reply, "What does renaissance mean?"

"Renaissance literally means rebirth," Pietro Agnesi replied, smiling at his daughter's enthusiasm. "The last few centuries have witnessed a renewed interest in the art, philosophy and science of classical antiquity. And that is why we are here Maria, to witness the influence of the ancient Greek philosophers on the evolution of human thought and world culture. The term Renaissance was first used in 1550 by Vasari, an art historian, to describe this revival."

In the *Stanze di Raffaello,* Pietro and his daughters admired the great works of Raphael. Pietro was particularly enthusiastic about *The School of Athens,* pointing out the two central figures engaged in philosophical discussion as Aristotle and Plato. Each has a book in his hands: Aristotle holds *Nicomachean Ethics* and Plato his *Timaeus.* In the same painting are also Pythagoras, Socrates, Euclid and Parmenides.

Maria was mesmerized by the *School of Athens*. She stood before it, absorbing its theme and message as she carefully examined each of the famous figures depicted in the painting. And then she noticed the image of a pale and slender woman standing behind Parmenides.

"Who is that, father? That lady behind Par...Para...," Maria trailed off.

"Parmenides," Pietro smiled.

"Yes, that is what I meant, father. Who is that woman in white clothes behind him?" asked Maria.

Pietro said he did not know but she was probably a student at the school of ancient Greek philosophy. Maria continued to scan the faces in the painting but her eyes were repeatedly drawn to the unknown woman in the white robe. She seemed disinclined to move away and Pietro had to remind her that it was almost nightfall and that they must return to their inn as they were due to leave for Milan early the next morning.

When Maria returned home after the trip to Rome, there was a change in her. She was quieter and not as playful as she used to be. She spent less time in the garden with Teresa and would sit for hours by the window in her room looking out, deep in thought.

"What has happened to our dear little child, Pietro?" Maria's parents were concerned about the change in her and felt that she had become too intense and serious for an eight year old.

"I do not know, Anna. Perhaps Rome and all the wonderful things she saw there left a deep impression on her. Do not worry, I am sure she will return to her usual self in a few days and spend her time playing in the garden with Teresa."

The following morning, Maria woke up before sunrise and went to her parents' room. Her father was surprised to see her up so early.

"What is the matter, Maria? Are you well?"

"I had a strange dream, father. I wish to tell you about it," Maria said as she settled down comfortably next to Pietro. "In my dream I was walking through an enormous room filled with shelves from floor to ceiling that were stacked with rolls of parchment, lit up by small lamps that hung from the ceiling. There were people in that room reading these scrolls and a group of them approached me and unrolled a large sheet of parchment. Their eyes filled with excitement as they poured over it and spoke to me in a language that I do not understand. There was something written on a wall in a strange script, but somehow I knew that it said that this was 'the place of the cure of the soul'."

"It was just a dream, Maria," Pietro was concerned and tried to reassure his daughter, "I hope that you were not afraid."

"Not at all, father. It was a very pleasant dream. I felt happy, almost elated, and at peace in that place. It seemed like a very dear place to me. And when I woke up, I felt so refreshed and invigorated."

After that, Maria developed a sudden fondness for books. She spent most of her time in her father's library reading philosophy, mathematics and natural sciences meant for much older readers. She also devoted her time to learning Latin as she believed that most of the really interesting books were written in that language.

And from time to time, Maria would be woken up early in the morning by her dreams that were always in the same unknown city that somehow felt familiar to her; a city with roads of stone with chariots on them; and open air markets selling scents, silks, silverware and spices brought from distant lands; and of people who wore long colourful robes in unfamiliar styles.

Pietro and Anna did not understand the meaning of Maria's dreams or why they recurred so frequently but since they did not seem to trouble her, they decided that they were harmless and that they need not worry about them.

About a year after her trip to Rome, Maria dreamt that she stood before a large gathering speaking to them on the philosophy of Plato. The crowd was full of men of different ages who listened intently to her long, eloquent speech. She felt power coming from her voice and her mind; the power to influence other minds, to make them understand the most complex of problems.

When Maria awoke in the morning she immediately went in search of Pietro.

"Father, may I deliver a speech at one of your academic evenings?" she asked enthusiastically.

After his initial astonishment, Pietro said, "Maria, I know that you have been reading extensively in my library and I appreciate your desire to speak in front of my guests but remember that these are highly educated men, some of whom teach at the University in Bologna. How can I presume that my young daughter will be able to speak before such an illustrious gathering of academics? They will think that I have invited them to show off my child's excellent classical education."

"Oh Father, I know I can do it. There is so much I can speak about - so much."

Maria felt compelled to speak in front of an audience willing to listen and understand.

"And what if you become the laughing stock of the evening? I don't want you to be discouraged by their comments on your attempt."

Maria hesitated and then said decisively, "Father, I will prepare a talk and only when you are satisfied with it, will I speak before your guests."

"A talk on what, Maria?"

"On Plato's philosophy."

Pietro burst out laughing, "What do you know about Plato, Maria?"

"Father, I *will* give a lecture on Plato to the members of your academic circle."

Maria's confidence returned and her eyes showed an unmistakable spirit of determination as she uttered these words, "I will give it only when you think that I am prepared to give it. Till then I will study and learn all I can about Plato and his philosophy."

Pietro did not have an answer to Maria's proposal. He nodded his head. Somewhere from deep inside him rose a feeling that Maria would succeed in her audacious ambition. It defied all logic and sense, and yet he knew that his eight-year-old daughter would do what she had promised with such determination.

From that day on Maria spent almost her entire day in her father's library. She was so engrossed that at times she would forget her meals. This worried Anna and she complained to Pietro that this was not natural in a child so young and he should not encourage her. Pietro, however, continued to help his daughter in her endeavour. If she forgot to come to the dining table for meals, he would himself take some soup and bread to Maria in the library. Sometimes Maria would be so tired that she would fall asleep as she poured over her books and Pietro would come each night at about midnight to check on her. He would remove her shoes and cover her with a blanket and then look at the books open on the table. He would smile at his daughter's flight into the glorious heights of intellectual ecstasy.

It was 24th July 1727, and in the large drawing room were gathered philosophers, mathematicians, men of science, and artists. As usual, Pietro's guests enjoyed conversing with their peers on a wide variety of topics and appreciated the delicious food and wine served at the Agnesi villa. And then Pietro made an announcement:

"Gentlemen, I hope you are enjoying the evening. I have a very special announcement. My daughter wishes to give a talk on a topic that she has prepared. I understand that you all have an immense amount of knowledge and so you may choose not to listen to my nine-year-old daughter. She will stand in this corner of the room to speak, so please listen to her only if you find her speech interesting. Maria, come here please…"

The guests were astonished that Pietro Agnesi would permit a nine-year-old girl to deliver a lecture to such an intellectual audience. As Pietro had predicted, many believed that it was to flaunt his daughter's education.

Renaissance

Little Maria walked over to the corner of the room and stood before the crowd. Nervously, she announced, "I will talk about Plato's views on the education of women as expressed in *The Republic,*" and then she began to speak in Latin. As she continued, her voice gained a power and force that drew the guests to the corner where she was speaking. They were amazed at the depth of her knowledge, her confidence, and her command of Latin.

As Maria spoke, she felt that she had found herself. She spoke like someone who had spent her life in the fire of intellectual zest. She spoke like a master teaching her students. She spoke with the ferociousness of someone who will defend every point that she has made.

Pietro stood to one side of the room listening and a tear of pride flowed down his cheek. He understood now that his daughter had within her heart a force that would take her to the heights of intellectual ecstasy. Through his daughter, Pietro would experience the joy of learning, and the sublime pleasure it brings to the mind.

Maria grew into a beautiful young woman. She dazzled with the radiance of her face, the sweetness of her voice and her sharp features. However, she dressed simply in plain clothes because, for Maria, the beauty of her face was meaningless. It was merely an image that hid something far more beautiful: the mind.

Since her first lecture when she was child, Maria had spoken often at her father's gatherings. In fact, these evenings had become famous in academic circles all over

Italy, and guests looked forward to being invited to them to listen to Maria. She had the ability to present the most complex philosophical or mathematical topic in such a way that everyone, from the novice to the expert, felt enlightened at the end of the lecture.

As she grew older, Maria's strange dreams continued. Sometimes she felt that she was leading a double life, one in Milan and another in a foreign city in a different age. Many features of these dreams would recur: she would often sit with an old and kindly man she called her father writing a long text on mathematics.

One night, the same old man appeared in her dream and wrote something on a piece of paper, and then she laughed as he recited a poem to her. As soon as she woke up she clearly remembered the mathematical equation the old man had written down:

$$x^3 - y^3 = c^3 + d^3$$

And she could repeat the first two lines of the poem although she had forgotten the rest of it:

> 'Here lies Diophantus,' the wonder behold.
> Through art algebraic, the stone tells how old.

The following day, Maria searched the library, which was now more hers than her father's, to see if she could find any reference to someone named Diophantus. She was amazed when she discovered that a mathematician of the

Renaissance

same name had lived in ancient Alexandria. However, her library did not yield any more information so she decided that she would visit the University of Bologna the following day to see if she could find out more about him.

The librarian at the university immediately found her a commentary on Diophantine algebra by Theon Alexandricus and Hypatia. She was disappointed to discover that it was in Greek, a language she did not know. But learning new languages had never been difficult for Maria. By the time she was thirteen, she knew French, Latin, Hebrew, German and Spanish, in addition to Italian, her mother tongue. Maria decided to take the book home with her and immediately began learning Greek.

In two weeks time she had gained mastery over Greek and eagerly opened the book she had borrowed from the university library. She had only read a few pages when a mathematical equation leapt off the page:

$$x^3 - y^3 = c^3 + d^3$$

Maria nearly dropped the book. She could hardly believe that this was the same equation that she remembered from her dream. As she read on, she was even more astonished to find the poem that the old man had recited in her dream. She now understood that it was one of Diophantus' mathematical problems written in verse:

'Here lies Diophantus,' the wonder behold.
Through art algebraic, the stone tells how old:
'God gave him his boyhood one-sixth of his life,
One twelfth more as youth while whiskers grew rife;
And then yet one-seventh ere marriage begun;
In five years there came a bouncing new son.
Alas, the dear child of master and sage
After attaining half the measure of his father's life
chill fate took him. After consoling his fate by the science of numbers for four years, he ended his life.'

Maria sat lost in thought, trying to fathom the strangeness of her experience. She had read so extensively throughout her life from such a young age and she tried to recall when and where she may have come across references to Diophantus. She must have, at some point over the years, read about Alexandria and its great library and the scholars who had lived there. She decided that this learning had made an impact on her that she had retained at a subconscious level, and which had manifested in her dreams.

About two months after this, Maria lectured on Diophantine equations at one of her father's academic gatherings. However, she continued to wonder about the characters who appeared so frequently in her dreams and was curious to find out more about the authors of the book that she had borrowed from the university library.

Maria decided to continue her research and returned once again to the library in Bologna to try to find out more about Theon and Hypatia. She spent the entire day there but was unable to find anything other than the book they had written together on Diophantine algebra that she had already read. Disappointed, she was about to give up her search when she came upon a pile of dusty manuscripts at the end of a row of shelves. She pulled one gently out of the pile. It was yellowed and torn with only a few chapters that were still partially legible. Its title was *The Mathematicians of Alexandria*. Maria could not believe her luck and settled down at once to read it.

The first few pages contained a description of Alexandria, a beautiful city of palaces and a great lighthouse that guided ships to this centre of learning that carried the philosophical traditions of the school of Athens. And at the heart of this culture was the great library. Maria gasped with surprise as she read about the ancient library, its magnificent exterior and its shelves of manuscripts; she knew that it was the same great building that appeared in her dreams. Most unsettling of all, she learned that it was known as "a place for the cure of the soul".

Maria carefully turned the fragile leaves of the document, frustrated that so many of the pages were damaged or missing. Finally, she was rewarded for her painstaking perseverance when she read a section that informed her that Hypatia was Theon's daughter and that together they had studied and taught at the great library in Alexandria. Maria was amazed and moved to learn that Hypatia was the first woman mathematician and that she had lived more than 1200 years before Maria was born.

The library was Hypatia's favourite place and her sanctuary from the world of men and women who liked to pass their time with gossip, eating and merriment. Hypatia only wished to teach these men and women that there is immense beauty and ecstatic pleasure in intellectual pursuits.

So, she ventured onto the streets of Alexandria giving lectures on philosophy and mathematics. Her teaching became popular and she was successful in her ambition as many of her listeners developed an interest in pursuits of the mind.

But popularity was not important to Hypatia. She wished only to spend her days pouring over scrolls in the great library, writing with her father, and teaching on the streets. Hypatia and her father wrote about the works of Euclid and Diophantus, and also of Ptolemy and Apollonius. It was a beautiful and happy life devoted to learning, thinking and teaching.

Once she had read through all the pages that were still legible, Maria went in search of the librarian to ask him if there was another copy of the manuscript so that she could finish reading the parts that were damaged or missing. He told her that the manuscript had been handwritten in the 8th century and, as far has he knew, only two copies had ever been made. She had just been reading one of them and he did not know the whereabouts of the second one, if it even existed.

Although she ached to know what was written on those missing pages, Maria was satisfied as she rode home in her carriage. She was thrilled to find a woman so far back in time yet who was so ahead of her time, as Maria was herself. She felt joy at having discovered another woman mathematician whose life strangely mirrored her own. She smiled to herself as she imagined the power that Hypatia felt while lecturing on philosophy and mathematics. Maria had felt the same power while speaking at her father's gatherings. She felt drawn to the historical Hypatia, as though she had found a friend 1200 years back in history, a friend who perhaps felt the same intellectual joy in philosophy and mathematics, a friend she would never meet. These thoughts put a warm glow of happiness in Maria's heart.

Her dreams had never troubled her but now she welcomed them and ceased to wonder why they came to her. She reasoned simply that during all the hours that she had spent pouring over her books, she had read about the places and historical figures that appeared so often in her dreams.

As the years passed Pietro became increasingly concerned about finding Maria a suitable husband; women from her background were expected to marry well. She had many admirers and offers of marriage from both rich and intellectual suitors from Milanese society.

But Maria turned them all down without meeting any of them. Pietro did not understand what she was looking for in a future husband, and Maria was becoming increasingly annoyed by her father's constant reference to the subject of her marriage, a subject she tried to avoid.

One night she dreamt that she stood beside the sea in a silk dress that shimmered in the moonlight. A man stood before her as he professed undying love for her. She turned away from the sea and spoke to him, telling him that there was nothing beautiful about love, that it merely springs from carnal desires and therefore has no lasting greatness or beauty. The man begged her to marry him or at least to permit him to be her lifelong slave. She replied that if he wished to be enslaved then he should choose something more worthy like philosophy or mathematics, and not a mere woman with good features. The man wept as she turned and walked back towards the imposing building where she liked to spend her days amongst the shelves of scrolls.

As soon as she woke up that morning, Maria went in search of her father and told him that she would never marry. Pietro was very upset and tried to persuade her to change her mind, reasoning that it was the correct thing for a woman of her class to do. Maria pointed out that it was also acceptable for a woman of her social position to become a nun. This course of action was even more unacceptable to her father. Maria then offered a solution: she would not become a nun if her father never raised the subject of marriage again. Furthermore, she would choose the gatherings she wished to attend and the people she wished to meet. Pietro reluctantly agreed.

Ten years had passed since this decisive period and Maria was now an established mathematician and philosopher. She had written *Instituzioni analitiche ad uso della gioventù italiana* which was immediately recognized all over Europe as the best introduction and exposition to the works of Euler, the great Swiss mathematician. In another manuscript, she discussed a mathematical curve which she described using an algebraic equation. To find an interesting name for this curve, she turned to her favourite language, Latin, and called it *versiera* derived from *vertere*, to turn.

Maria's mother had died several years earlier and Pietro was not in good health. Maria devoted herself to study and to caring for her sick father. She would walk down the stairs from her library almost every half hour to see her father, and to make sure that he was being given good food to eat and that he was taking his medicines on time. She would spend almost her entire day in her library reading, writing and thinking. She never felt lonely: her greatest love, the world of books and knowledge, was always her trusted companion.

She was recognized by Pope Benedict XIV who appointed her professor at the University of Bologna. She had always been well known in Italy but her fame spread throughout Europe; people wanted to know about the first woman to write a book on mathematics in over a thousand years, and the first woman professor at a university.

Maria was unaffected by this fame. She remained absorbed in her books and work and the care of her dying father. One day, she learned through a friend that John Colson, a mathematician at Cambridge University, England, had translated her work and had named the mathematical curve in the book "The Witch of Agnesi".

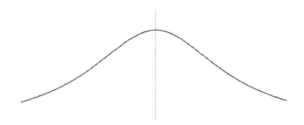

The Witch Of Agnesi

"Witch, why witch?" Maria wondered.

"Because the word *versiera* is close to the word *avversier*, or she-devil," her friend replied.

"Similar does not mean same! Surely there must be words in English which sound similar but have different meanings," Maria sounded distressed. "He knew enough Italian to translate my book but changed that one word to mean witch, and named the curve "The Witch of Agnesi"! He is a professor at Cambridge, could he not have asked someone in the department of Latin at his university? Or he could have written to me to ask me what *versiera* means?"

"He knows enough Italian to translate the book. I am sure that he knew the meaning of *versiera*. Perhaps he just wanted to have some fun at your expense. Maybe he did it deliberately because he was jealous of you, your intellectual abilities and your fame," her friend tried to find an explanation.

That night as she lay on her bed, she tried hard to sleep but her mind kept going back to "The Witch of Agnesi." She wondered why this incident had distressed her so much. Maria had always lived in the closed and secure world of her home, her library and books, and her family. She had been taught at home by tutors and her only contact with the outside world was through her father's academic evenings. Someone of her serious nature found the frivolous title upsetting, but that was not the only reason. She had always been a deeply religious woman and the allusion to witches and its derogatory connotations upset her greatly. *Is a woman who loves mathematics a witch?* she wondered as she lay on her bed, *Can a woman be nothing more than a wife and a mother? Are men not able to accept that a woman can love knowledge and think about philosophy?* Her mind was filled with such questions as she tossed and turned on her bed for several hours. And then, well past midnight, sleep came to her.

Almost at once she fell into the now familiar world of her dreams but this time she was gripped by terror. She was soaked in blood and howling in pain. Blood stained the street outside the great hall that was so dear to her. She was surrounded by a crowd of frenzied men who reached out to grab her. Overcome with dread, she woke up.

Covered with sweat and with her heart pounding, she tried to understand the meaning of her nightmare. For so many years now, these dreams had been her sanctuary from the mundane routine of the real world. In them, she had found inspiration on how life should be lived. But today, for the first time, she had woken up mortally terrified.

By late evening, she felt calmer, convinced that her dreams were merely a reflection of her mood on a particular day. She decided that if she went to bed in a happier frame of mind, her dreams would also be more pleasant. As she dropped off to sleep, Galileo's *Dialogue Concerning Two World Systems* slipped from her hands.

Almost at once she saw herself in the familiar streets of her dreams, riding in a chariot on her way to the great hall which was her beloved place in that city.

Ahead of her, on her customary route, she saw a mob of wild, angry men. Not sure what the commotion was, she instructed her charioteer to take another route. Without warning, the men surged towards her and surrounded her. She was pulled from her seat and held as her clothes were torn from her body until she was completely naked. She was revolted by the expression in the men's eyes, a mixture of lust and hatred, and she begged them to spare her. A large crowd gathered to watch the fate of the woman who lectured so passionately about philosophy and mathematics.

Her naked body was cut by stones as the frenzied men dragged her through the streets. She shrieked with pain as her body traced a path of blood across the cobblestones. The mob finally stopped in front of a building that looked to be a place of worship. There, using sharp oyster shells, they tore her skin to pieces.

Just as she knew she could not stand anymore and that life must leave her, Maria awoke from her nightmare, sobbing bitterly. It was still dark but she could no longer sleep, disgusted and terrified by her dream. She tried to tell herself that it was only a nightmare, and when her breathing slowed and she felt calmer, she sat in a chair in her room to think about what she had experienced.

She felt that, in some way, these dreams had a meaning. She had experienced them since she had been a very little girl. As her mind wandered, the painting that had made such an impression on her during her first trip to Rome sprang clearly into her mind: it was *The School of Athens*. She got up at once and went to find her father. She told him that she would visit the Vatican and return the following day.

The School of Athens had always been a painting that she deeply cherished. As she stood before it, her eyes immediately went to the image of the woman who stood behind Parmenides. As she continued to stare at the figure in white, she felt a strange pull, as though she had some connection to this painted image.

Slowly, she turned away from the masterpiece but now she knew what she must do. She had to find out the identity of the woman in the painting.

The following morning after she had checked on her father, she returned to the library in Bologna. She found plenty of information on Raphael and quickly learned the identities of all the figures depicted in *The School of Athens*. Maria's eyes filled with tears as she read:

And standing behind Parmenides, in white clothes symbolizing purity of body and soul, is the first woman mathematician, Hypatia.

Deeply moved and lost in thought, Maria was startled by a tap on her shoulder. It was the same librarian who had helped her all those years ago, although he was an old man now. He smiled at Maria and said, "I see that you are still fascinated by ancient Alexandria. Well, I have something for you. You may remember that I told you there were only two copies of the ancient manuscript which you found so interesting. Well, I was clearing out the basement a few months ago and I found the second copy. Furthermore, it is perfectly preserved. I was hoping that you would come to the library so that I could show it to you."

Maria smiled gratefully at the old man and turned eagerly to the manuscript. Although its pages were yellowed and fragile, they were intact. She gently leafed through it until she came to the section about Theon and Hypatia and read on.

Renaissance

Maria learned that change had come to Alexandria. A new religion was spreading amongst the people, a religion that valued devotion to their God more than the quest for knowledge. In fact, the intellectual search for truth was discouraged as it was seen as questioning the will and intention of God. Furthermore, it was opposed to the education of women as it was believed that women lost their purity when they become intelligent. This new religion was called Christianity.

Its followers were jealous of Hypatia's popularity. At first, they tried to spread false rumours about her moral character calling her an evil woman, whore, and even a witch. This had little effect because those who knew of Hypatia and had heard her speak understood that she had dedicated her life to learning and that her moral character was beyond reproach. And so, in desperation, these followers of the new faith caused her brutal death.

Hypatia believed that the way to gain wisdom was by questioning and doubt. She was a woman who spent her life wanting to grow in knowledge rather than devoting it to her husband. She was murdered because of this, and because when she spoke, people listened and followed. Because she, a woman, could do what these men could not. Her killers feared her quest for the truth and hid behind a curtain of ignorance claiming that it was the wish of their God.

Maria came home deeply disturbed by what she had read. For the first time in her life, she was afraid to close her eyes, afraid of what her dreams would reveal. That night, she tossed and turned and eventually towards dawn, fell into a fitful sleep.

The victorious mob built a fire and threw Hypatia into its flames and stood by as her body burned, shouting slogans to mark their victory over the evil they had destroyed. Her pain ended as life left her torn and naked body.

Maria was heartbroken. She knew that the only way to find peace was to make the trip to the Vatican.

In the *Stanze di Raffaello,* she stood quietly in front of the painting that had had such an impact on her life. Her eyes fixed on the figure in white who had come to mean so much to her, Maria spoke softly:

"I do not know whether I am you, born again more than one thousand years later. Or whether somehow, subliminally, I have absorbed your story from all the books I have read in my life. My life has been golden and blessed and I have been recognised and feted for what I have achieved. Long ago, my father told me that renaissance means rebirth. I now know that I have been born to carry forward the torch that was snatched away from you."

With Hypatia's death, the spirit of enquiry was extinguished and the world plunged into the dark ages. For more than 1200 years this spirit waited to be born again. With time, the world that had descended into darkness emerged once again into light. But the light of knowledge is not complete until women also bathe in it and add to its brilliance. So Hypatia's spirit continued to wait.

Renaissance

And then this spirit of enquiry found Maria. This is was Hypatia's rebirth. This was Hypatia's renaissance!

Hypatia was the first notable woman mathematician. She became the head of the Platonist school and lectured on the philosophy of Plato and Aristotle to students from all over the world who came to study at the great library of Alexandria. Hypatia collaborated with her father, Theon Alexandricus, to produce some major works on philosophy and mathematics. She edited Euclid's Elements, Diophantus' Arithmetica *and* Ptolemy's Almagest.

Though she had many suitors, she rebuffed them all, telling them that there is nothing beautiful about carnal desires. She never married and remained a virgin throughout her life.

In March 415 AD she was attacked and murdered by a mob of Christian monks who accused her of being a pagan and of causing religious turmoil. They dragged her through the streets of Alexandria, stripped her naked, and set her ablaze while she was still alive. The great library of Alexandria was also burnt at about that time.

Maria Agnesi lived in the 18th century and was a mathematician and philosopher and an extraordinary linguist; by the age of thirteen she was fluent in Greek, German, Latin, Hebrew and, of course, Italian. She *wrote the first book that discussed both differential and integral calculus and several fundamental texts on mathematics. She is most famous for the curve known as the* Witch of Agnesi.

She was the first woman professor at a university: she was appointed professor at the University of Bologna by the pope.

She was beautiful and had many suitors but she refused all of them.

The death of Hypatia was symbolic of the extinguishing of the light of classical antiquity and the beginning of the dark ages in Europe. This darkness lasted till the love of knowledge and the arts that was central to classical antiquity was reborn during the period that came to be known as the Renaissance.

The Present

O Time! the beautifier of the dead,
Adorner of the ruin, comforter
And only healer when the heart hath bled--
Time! the corrector where our judgments err,
The test of truth, love, sole philosopher,
For all besides are sophists, from thy thrift
Which never loses though it doth defer--
Time, the avenger! unto thee I lift
My hands, and eyes, and heart, and crave of thee a gift.

From "Childe Harold's Pilgrimage" by LORD BYRON

The Double Helix

Year 1990

Akanksha Talwar and Arti Pandit had been friends ever since they could remember. They were always together to the extent that their teachers and classmates referred to them with a single name, Arti-Akanksha. They were both good students, not top of their class but always in the first twenty. They were obedient girls and tried to impress their teachers with their hard work and diligence.

When they were in the 8th standard, a new biology teacher joined the school. Ashok Trivedi was a great teacher and quickly won the admiration of what was generally considered the most mischievous class in school. Within a week of joining, he described Mendel's laws of genetics and went on to tell the class about a very interesting book about the scientific adventure that led to the discovery of the double helix structure of DNA. Both Arti and Akanksha wanted to make a good impression on the new 'sir' so they bought the book with great excitement and decided to begin reading it the same night so that they would finish it within one week. They then wanted to write a book review to impress 'sir'.

"Sir will be so amazed," said Arti.

"Yes, and he might read our book review in front of the whole class!" exclaimed Akanksha.

A new book always tempts and excites, the freshness of its pages, its smell and feel intoxicate so that the reader thinks he will skim through it in no time. However, it is easier to buy a book than to read it. After the first few pages, it loses its crispness and then the battle begins between, on one hand, the will to master the content and, on the other, page after page of information that is hard to grasp and sentences that are difficult to understand.

It is this battle that Arti and Akanksha faced with full fury that night. Both went to bed after having read the first few pages, promising that they would read more the next day. But as the days passed they made no progress and the books lay unopened where they had left them. They began to avoid discussing it with each other, convinced that the other had read more of it. They were both miserable at their failure and wished that they had never embarked on their mission to read *The Double Helix* and write a book review to impress 'sir'.

Shortly after this, Arti received a phone call from her cousin Pankaj who lived in Lajpat Nagar. He was planning a birthday party for his father and wanted to invite Arti and her parents. Arti accepted the invitation and as she turned to leave her room, her eyes fell on the book that she had been struggling so hard to read. Arti's uncle was a voracious reader and she had the sudden idea that *The Double Helix* would be an ideal gift for him. With this thought, she felt happy and light; relieved of the enormous weight of expectation she had placed on herself. She had dealt with the situation and the book would no longer haunt her.

At the birthday party, Arti presented her gift to Pankaj's father beautifully wrapped in gold paper. He opened it in front of everyone and was delighted, "Hey, I have wanted to buy this book myself. How thoughtful of you to gift it to me, Arti," he exclaimed. Everyone at the party admired Arti's choice of birthday present and Arti felt great. The approval of people dear to her and the fact that she felt that she had done something nice for someone else made the decision to give her uncle *The Double Helix* worthwhile. Without the book to remind her, she could now push her feeling of failure at being unable to read it to the back of her mind. However, what is at the back of one's mind is still in the mind, and often it is hard to understand the effect these suppressed feelings have on us.

Akanksha was having a much more difficult time dealing with her inability to make progress with the book and it seemed to mock her whenever she went to her room. She began to feel a failure and that hurt her. One day, out of frustration, she picked it up again, sat at her desk and started reading it slowly, sentence by sentence. After a few pages she became interested in the story of Watson and Crick and began to break through the barrier that had prevented her from reading more than the first few pages. She was making great progress and began to enjoy the story of the amusing and competitive world of scientific research that was so different from the heroic aspect of science they were taught in school about such great men as Galileo and Archimedes. Akanksha now read a few pages before going to bed and the number increased each night as her interest grew. The fascinating world of books had inducted one more amazed member into its fold.

Akanksha finished the book in a few weeks. It was like a personal triumph and she revelled in it for days. She had completed a task that she had been afraid of and had read the book that no one in her class, apart from Arti, had even bought. She was proud of herself. 'Sir' himself read her review of *The Double Helix* to the class. She stood out, she was different, and she felt that she was more intelligent than rest of the class. Arti applauded along with the rest of her classmates but her feelings were a mixture of awe and misery. She had failed at the same task but she did not want to accept it. So she told herself that, instead of selfishly enjoying the book and then arrogantly showing off about it in front of everyone, she had been thoughtful and done something special for someone else.

It was a turning point. Akanksha's and Arti's interests and outlook on life slowly changed and they grew apart. Akanksha began taking more interest in her studies. She set tasks for herself and achieving them gave her great satisfaction. She had impressed the biology teacher and she worked hard to stay in favour with him. She worked particularly hard on biology and topped the class in that subject in her next exam.

Arti, on the other hand, lost interest in her school work and made friends with a group who did not do well in class. They were more fun to be with and although they may not have been high achievers, she found them friendlier and more caring than the academically bright ones like Akanksha.

And one day, Akanksha and Arti had an argument. It was about something minor; Arti accused Akanksha of not returning her call the previous evening but like many trivial arguments, it took an ugly turn as both brought up grievances unrelated to the issue that began the fight. Once a disagreement degenerates into attacks on one another's personalities, it gets magnified beyond recognition. Arti accused Akanksha of arrogance and Akanksha said Arti had become boring and that she was jealous of Akanksha's achievements. The fight became so ugly that both decided never to talk to each other again.

Year 1994

Akanksha was preparing hard for her medical entrance examinations. She had no doubt that the following year she would be in medical college. The only question was: which one? She had set her sights on AIIMS and she knew that it was extremely difficult to gain admission. But she told herself that about fifty intelligent and hardworking students would join the premier medical school in India and there was no reason why she should not be amongst them. *Akanksha* means desire and ambition and she would not be doing justice to herself and her name if she did not aim high. She hung a photograph of AIIMS over her desk and looked at it whenever she felt exhausted and needed motivation after endless hours of studying physics, chemistry and biology.

Arti had always been good at drawing. She would spend hours sketching her teachers and fellow students in the back of her exercise books. Her father had suggested that, as she was good at art, architecture may be the right profession for her. Arti never doubted her father, he always knew what was best for her, and she agreed that architecture may be interesting. So, after she had passed her 10th standard exams, she began preparing for the entrance examination to the Delhi School of Planning and Architecture.

Arti was no longer amongst the top twenty in her class and continued to perform poorly in tests. She knew it was extremely difficult to obtain a place at the DSPA and she became convinced that she would not be able to get in and had almost given up any hope of doing so. Afraid of what others might think, she continued to behave as though she was confident she would make it through the entrance exams. If she told them that she had given up, she felt that they would say that she had done so because she knew she would fail. She found it hard to admit to herself that she was a failure.

The Double Helix

Arti's brother, Amit, was preparing for his 10th class examinations and everyone in the family had very high expectations of him. Arti loved her brother and started showering him with care; she cooked all his favourite dishes and made tea for him late at night to help him stay awake and study. She would buy him "best of luck" cards before every class test. She felt happy doing that. She spent all her time taking care of her hard working brother and neglected her own study. Amit was grateful and would tell her that it was thanks to her that he was able to concentrate so well. Arti's parents had higher expectations of their son and placed the weight of their ambition on his shoulders. Although they expected Arti to continue with her education, they were more concerned that she was considered a kind and caring person.

Arti was happy helping Amit and proud of the sacrifices she made for him. She would never admit to herself that it was a way to escape the disappointment of her own failure to excel academically. It was easier to let go of her aspirations and help her brother who had a greater chance of success. That way, it would appear that she had sacrificed her own goals in order to help her brother succeed and she would bask in the glory of having a hand in his success. Personal failure is painful so rather than risk it, it is easier to hide behind the facade of selfless service to others.

Shadows of Lost Time

Year 2006

Dr Akanksha Talwar was one of the best neurosurgeons in Delhi. She was an MBBS from Maulana Azad Medical College, one of the top medical colleges in Delhi. Most medical students would consider a place at Maulana Azad a great achievement but not Akanksha. She had been miserable throughout her five-year course. For her, the world began and ended with AIIMS. So, for her post graduate degree, she applied only to AIIMS and no other college. She was accepted, became a neurosurgeon, and decided to stay on there to practice. The most difficult and complex cases were referred to her. She was very successful.

But Dr Akanksha Talwar was not happy. Her marriage to Dr Vikram Chaturvedi was in shambles. They fought almost every day over the smallest things. Invariably, it was Vikram who would have to apologise and beg her to calm down.

He had been in love with her since their college days when they were both studying for their MBBS. Even then, Akanksha had been difficult. Her arrogance and volatile temperament combined with her exceptional beauty made her one of the most sought after girls in college. Vikram had pursued her for two years and when she eventually agreed to a relationship, it felt like a great victory to him. He had no idea what was in store. The qualities that he had once found attractive became extremely hard to live with once they were married. Akanksha always put her own interests first and Vikram had found this endearing when they were in college. She had been his goddess but he discovered that you cannot marry a goddess. When Akanksha climbed down off her pedestal to marry him, his expectations changed. He wanted his partner to be on equal terms in their relationship and Akanksha slowly wore out the characteristics that had made him fall in love with her. Those same traits were now major irritants for Vikram and members of his family. Their marriage was two years old but already some of their fights ended with threats of divorce.

Akanksha wanted to make her marriage work but the challenge was so different from the ones she had conquered in the past. Preparing for examinations and getting great grades was something tangible and easy to understand, but other people and their unpredictable needs and emotions provided no clear blueprint to follow and offered no clear measure of success. Indeed, the definition of success in a relationship was nothing like the success she strove for in her career. She had planned and done her best to succeed and this had lead to landmarks of recognition in her field. But she wondered at what point she would be able to declare her marriage a success. There would be no single crowning day of achievement to mark her accomplishment. Each day, the marriage brought new challenges that needed understanding, wisdom and adjustment and the need to recognise the individuality of the other person. Akanksha had no idea what she could do differently, and that lead to great disharmony.

Shadows of Lost Time

Arti Pandit had married Vikas Gaur five years back and they had two lovely children. Theirs was a typical Indian arranged marriage. Arti had changed her name to Arti Gaur and did her best to be a great wife, a great mother, and a great daughter-in-law. According to Indian custom, they were a joint family: Arti and her husband as well as Vikas' brother and his wife and children, lived in Vikas' parents' house. Arti was very popular with her in-laws; they were all fond of her and thought of her as a nice, selfless and caring person.

Arti spent her day taking care of her family and she was always there for anyone who needed her, ready with support or if they wanted someone to talk to. Because she was constantly available, they became dependent on her, and her family considered her the ideal woman. Even her mother-in-law frequently held her up as an example of selfless care; someone who placed the interests of others before her own. However, at the end of the day, Arti would be emotionally and physically exhausted. Sometimes, as she lay drained and weary on her bed, she would imagine what life may have been like if she had become an architect and had lived on her own terms. But sleep would soon overtake her and in the morning she would forget about these thoughts as she launched into her busy day.

One evening Arti was shopping in busy Khan Market when she saw a familiar face. Although she looked older now, Arti immediately recognised Akanksha. She was thrilled to see her and Akanksha was equally overjoyed at the meeting. They sat together and chatted over coffee at Barista, the fight of their school days completely forgotten. They talked about the happy times when they had been so similar in their habits and outlook that they had been inseparable. And they caught up on news about their families and where life had taken them after school. They lost track of time as they discovered how different their lives had become when they grew apart after their fight. But now they spoke as old friends; freely, openly, and without hesitation. They were back to the way they used to be before their fight. Friendship is often inexplicable; the reason why two people bond and are close is frequently beyond analysis. But whatever this seed of friendship is, both Arti and Akanksha discovered that it was still planted deep within them. Their fight had merely been an interruption. They were meant to be friends forever.

That night at dinner, everyone noticed that Arti was quiet. She seemed lost in thought. Later, she could not sleep and spent the entire night tossing and turning. For once, exhaustion at the end of the day did not prevent thoughts and emotions from tormenting her. She wondered why Akanksha and she had not remained friends. Would Akanksha have encouraged her to lead a more independent life? Akanksha was so successful but what did Arti have to show for years of selfless service to her family? She thought about her name: *Arti* - the act of worshipping a deity. She wondered if *arti* had an existence independent of the deity or whether *arti* existed solely to worship the deity. She wondered where, in the course of her life, she had lost her individuality.

Shadows of Lost Time

When she got up in the morning, she had made a decision. She told her husband she wanted to speak to him and their discussion almost lead to a fight. She wanted more time for herself to pursue her own interests. The rest of the family got to know of her uncharacteristic demands and worried that Arti was unwell. Her mother-in-law suggested to her son that he take her on a three-day holiday to Nainital. She said the change would do Arti good and she would return to her usual nice, happy, friendly nature.

The next day Arti went to a bookstore and bought *The Double Helix*. This time she knew that she would read it.

Akanksha had also spent the same night tormented by her thoughts. She wondered if her success had any value at all. She wondered why she had always placed herself before others. She wondered why her marriage was failing while Arti's was so successful.

When Akanksha woke up the next morning, the first thing she did was to turn to Vikram and say sorry for all the fights that they had ever had and for all the times when she had acted in an unreasonable manner. Vikram was astonished, he had never heard her apologise. For the first time, Vikram began to feel that Akanksha needed him and that she wanted things to be better between them. At last, he saw a ray of hope.

The Double Helix

Year 2009

It was a big day for Arti. Her first solo exhibition of paintings was to open at a gallery in the India Habitat Centre. Over the last three years, she had begun to paint and draw again and, little by little, she had spent more and more time on her art. This exhibition would reveal the effort and pleasure that she had put into her paintings. She was proud as she carefully checked that everything was in order and that the paintings were properly displayed.

All Arti's friends and relatives would be at the event. Her husband and in-laws had gradually accepted the change in her, and Vikas now took pride in her work. Her mother-in-law had expressed her approval by asking Arti to paint the battle scene from the *Mahabharata* in which Krishna gives the message of the *Gita* to Arjun. Arti managed to turn down the idea without hurting her mother-in-law's feelings by saying that she would only attempt to paint it when her talent had developed to the stage where she would be able to do justice to such a divine subject.

Her paintings, neatly hung and labelled, filled three walls of the gallery but the fourth wall that faced the guests as they entered was covered with a black curtain.

Akanksha phoned her to say that she would be late because Vikram and she had to attend a recital at her two-year-old son Neeraj's playschool.

Arti was delighted when the gallery quickly filled up with friends, family and strangers admiring her work. An hour into the event, Akanksha and Vikram walked in and she immediately went over and hugged Arti. A photographer asked them to pose together for a picture and they agreed happily.

Then Arti walked away to stand next to a cord that hung from the black curtain at the end of the room. She turned to address the assembled guests:

"Ladies and Gentlemen, thank you for sparing your precious time to come and see my paintings. I want to request my dear friend Akanksha to reveal my most beloved work."

Akanksha walked over to stand beside her and Arti held her hand and led her to the rope that hung from the black curtain. Akanksha pulled it and the curtain fell open to reveal an enormous painting that covered much of the wall. It was an image in oil of two entwined strands that seemed to flow as they spiralled round each other. The viewers quickly understood that the images depicted within one strand conveyed togetherness and interdependence, and within the other, the heart's unrestrained desire for self progress. One strand portrayed benevolence and kindness to others, and the other represented self and what is precious in one's own heart. But both strands were forever connected.

It was the double helix in which one-half stood for the self and the other stood for the world outside us.

Akanksha understood. There were tears in her eyes as she hugged Arti and said, "On that day when we met again after so many years, I realized that the secret of a happy and fulfilled life lies not in *akanksha* or *arti,* but a combination of the two. What is done for the self should balance what is done for others around us. You have depicted it perfectly as a double helix of human endeavour. It is beautiful!"

The caption next to the painting read: *The Double Helix* by Arti Pandit Gaur. Extremely precious. NOT FOR SALE.

Sunrise

16th April, 2009

Abhilasha is a multistorey apartment complex somewhere in East Delhi. It contains about two hundred flats, most of them two and three bedrooms each. It is late, 11.35 at night, and nearly all the lights in the building are turned off. But, light still glows through the bedroom window of a flat on the third storey. This bedroom is sparsely furnished; there is a double bed in the centre of the room, two chairs, a clock and an old radio. A woman in her early twenties lies on the bed with a pillow supporting her. Her long hair falls on her delicate shoulders. She wears a *salwar-kameez*. Her large eyes look intently at the man who sits on a chair next to her. They have been talking for hours and four empty cups from which they had drunk tea lie on the floor next to the bed.

"Why do you love me so much, Amir?" the woman asks.

Sunrise

Amir smiles. He cannot take his eyes off her, "Because I have no choice. And because there is nothing in the world as beautiful as you. Because, whenever I think about life, I think about you, Shabana. You have engulfed my mind, my heart, my soul, my being."

Shabana looks down shyly and smiles. "Maybe I cannot live up to the image that you have created of me. What if one day you realise that the image was false? What if love leaves your heart?"

"That will never happen, Shabana!" Amir replies forcefully, trying to rid Shabana of her fears. "The divine image that I have of you is true. The more I understand you, the more this vision seems real. In fact, you are more beautiful than any picture that can be conceived in my mind or the mind of any mortal being. My love for you cannot end. This world can end, this life can end but my love - never! I will love you forever."

"And I will be yours for ever. Yours and only yours," Shabana smiles.

They continue to gaze at each other. Even in silence, their eyes convey a thousand messages to the other. The radio plays on and strains of the old melodious song sung by Rafi fill the room:

Mujhko apne gale laga le, ai mere humrahi
Tumko kya batlaon main, ke tumse kitna pyaar hai.

Come take me in your arms, O my life's companion.

Shadows of Lost Time

How can words alone describe how much I love you?

Amir and Shabana are oblivious to the passing of time. They have been together for over four hours now. When the clock strikes twelve, Shabana wakes up from the stupor of the world of dreams.

"Amir, it is late! You must go home now."

"It is midnight already. Yes, I must leave."

"But how will you get home?" asks Shabana anxiously. "The Metro will not be running at this time."

"You are right. I guess I'll have to walk."

"Your house is far away. I cannot let you go out alone at this time."

"Wow, you love me so much, Shabana!" Amir says teasingly.

"Shut up, Amir," Shabana replies with mock severity. "Be serious. This is important."

Amir pulls a sad face, "I thought that love was the most important thing."

"I'm so sorry, my adorable Amir. Of course, love is the most important thing. But we must be practical and find a way for you to get home tonight. After that, you can talk about love - endlessly - as you always do," Shabana laughs.

"I think I will just go," Amir smiles at her.

"Don't go," Shabana's voice is soft and melodious.

"Okay, I won't."

"No. No. No. Go. Go home."

They both laugh. Then there is a long silence.

Sunrise

"Can I just stay here tonight?" Amir asks in a low, pleading tone.

"But...!" Shabana is surprised.

"You trust me, don't you?" asks Amir. "You know that I won't do anything stupid. We will just sleep here and I will go home tomorrow morning."

Shabana is quiet as she thinks about what Amir has just suggested.

"Okay," she says finally, "but what will I tell the maid if she comes early to clean the house and finds you here?" Shabana knows that the maid would be shocked.

"Send her away. Tell her you do not need any work done today. Come on Shabana! It is not every day that your roommates are away. And you know me; I will just lie next to you and sleep. You know me, Shabana."

Shabana falls silent but after some time she makes up her mind and smiles.

"Okay. But you can't touch me."

"You know me, Shabana," Amir repeats.

A while later, they lie down next to each other on the bed and Shabana turns off the light.

"This is the most beautiful night of my life," Amir whispers.

"Why, Amir?" Shabana laughs.

"Because I am lying next to my paradise, Shabana."

"Your words fill me with incredible happiness, Amir."

After a few moments, Amir stirs, "Can I place my hand on you? Please."

Shabana does not reply for some time.

"Okay," she speaks shyly, her voice faint.

Amir places his hand on her. Shabana puts her hand on his.

"I love you Shabana. I hope this night never ends."

"This night will end but there will be countless nights like this."

"Promise?"

"Promise."

They talk for a little while longer and then they both fall asleep.

As the sun rises the next morning, Amir opens his eyes and sees Shabana looking at him. She is smiling and her eyes convey endless adoration of him. He smiles at her. Shabana kisses Amir's hand.

"What will you have for breakfast?" she asks.

"Whatever you make for me, my love."

"I'll make you fried eggs," Shabana smiles as she heads for the kitchen.

"Thank you for the beautiful night. I feel as though a goddess has bestowed a great favour on an unworthy creature," Amir's eyes fill with tears.

Shabana rushes back to him and wipes his tears away.

"O Amir. I love you, I adore you. And I will love you forever. And this will never go away. And I will make sure that your eyes never have tears in them again after this day."

Shabana puts her arms around him and they embrace. Amir's eyes are still full of tears.

Sunrise

14th August, 2009

It is 11.15 at night. It is raining heavily outside. Amir and Shabana are in the same bedroom. Shabana is lying flat on the bed and looking up at the ceiling. Amir is looking at Shabana; his eyes convey worry and thoughtfulness.

"Shabana."

"What?"

"Why do you get so angry with me?"

Shabana stays silent.

"Why do you get so angry with me, Shabana?" Amir asks again. "What has happened to us?"

"I don't know," Shabana replies, her voice stern.

"It is okay if you don't know. But don't you want our love to return?"

"What love?"

"The love that we had for each other."

"I never loved you."

"Yes, you did, once."

Shabana is angry, "Do I know what I feel or used to feel or do *you* know what I feel? You may be intelligent, sir, but you cannot know my thoughts."

"But you said you loved me so many times."

"That was a mistake."

"No! It was not. Those were the most beautiful days of my life. Don't call them a mistake. Those days meant the world to me," Amir is agitated.

"Then keep those days, but leave me alone."

Amir continues to look at Shabana. Shabana looks at the ceiling. A long silence follows.

"Shabana, you used to be so different. You used to say so many things. You used to feel so much love for me. Why have you changed?"

"How do I know why things have changed? You claim to be well read, you tell me why feelings change. If you cannot tell me, go and find out and then tell me. Why do you ask me why I have changed? Do you think that I have decided to change? Don't ask me. Please don't ask me. That is all that you ever do. Ask. Ask. Ask. Can't you just feel?"

"I feel so sad when you talk to me like this."

"Stop it. Stop trying to make me feel guilty about things that I have no control over. I am not responsible for your misery. Do not try to make me feel guilty for your emotions."

There is another long silence.

"I love you, Shabana."

Shabana is irritated, "I know!"

"Why do you find everything that I say irritating?"

Shabana turns to look at Amir, "Maybe I am just irritated with myself for letting you come so close."

"You have lost interest in me because I am too predictable. You have lost interest in me because I love you and you know that I cannot leave you. You have taken me and my love for granted because you feel that you can never lose me."

Shabana stays silent.

Amir continues his analysis, "There are so many amazing things around us but we take them for granted. This massive Earth rotates on its axis every twenty-four hours and completes its huge circle around the sun every 365 days. And this has been happening for billions of years. How many people get amazed by these miracles of nature that happen every day? They just take them for granted and go about their lives. Why? Because they happen every day! They are predictable!

'Yet when there is a solar eclipse, look at the excitement it causes. The television and newspapers are full of it. Why? Because it is rare, and because it is temporary. It cannot be taken for granted.

'Love is like that too. To value it one has to fear its loss. You have no such fear. And my fear has become reality."

"So what can I do?" Shabana asks coldly. "What really is your problem? I have told you that I do not feel what I felt earlier. WHAT CAN I DO? I TRIED. GOD KNOWS THAT I TRIED. Please do not keep asking me so many questions. Please leave me alone!"

"We are friends, aren't we? Can't you just be friends?" she added.

"What is my problem?" Amir raises his voice, "I see my precious dream vanishing, piece by piece, that is my problem. My dream is breaking and so is my heart, slowly, painfully, and cruelly."

Shabana looks at him angrily and then turns her head away.

"The eyes that once looked at me with such love and adoration now look at me with anger and criticism. I am the same person. It is the eyes that have changed. And I hate this change."

Shabana says nothing and continues to stare at the ceiling. Amir keeps looking at Shabana. The battered radio plays an old melodious song by Rafi:

> *Dil ke mere paas ho itne, phir bho kitni door*
> *tum mujh se, main dil se pareshaan, donon hain majboor*
> *aise mein kisko kaun manaaye ?*

> You are so close to me, yet you are so far away.
> You are annoyed by me, I am disturbed by my heart,
> We cannot find a way.
> In this situation who will agree with whom?

The clock strikes twelve. Shabana is startled and immediately looks at Amir.

"You have to go home. It is late."

"Yes, I should."

"Yes, go now."

"But it is midnight. And the Metro trains are no longer running. And it is raining outside."

"The rain is not heavy. And you told me many times that you like to walk."

"Can't I just stay here? We will talk and I will sleep here. You know me. I will not do anything stupid."

Shabana shouts, "NO!"

Amir thinks back to the past, "Remember that beautiful night..."

"That was a mistake. People should not repeat mistakes."

"Do not call that a mistake," Amir speaks angrily, "that was the most beautiful night of my life. This night is a mistake."

"Bye Amir! Good night," Shabana is angry too.

Amir gets up, walks to the door, and opens it. Shabana is right behind him. The sound of rain falling on the road tells them about its intensity.

"It is raining hard," Amir says.

"I have ears. I know!"

Amir's eyes are full of hurt, "Bye, Shabana."

Shabana turns away.

Amir takes a step forward and the door immediately closes behind him, reflecting Shabana's feelings. The same door has closed countless times on Amir's departure. In the past, the door was closed as if to tell Amir that Shabana wanted to open it again the next day. Or that it was closed unwillingly. Or that it was closed with the hope that someday it would never have to close on Amir's departure again. But that was then. Today, the door closes brutally behind him and tells Amir that he should not even bother to look back.

Amir walks down the stairs and as soon as he reaches the ground floor, he goes out in the rain and tears start to flow down his cheeks. He places his hands on his face and weeps bitterly. He had been trying to control these tears for several hours now and is, in a way, relieved to be out of the house so that they can flow from his tired eyes. Their intensity seems to reflect the intensity of the rain that falls on Amir.

Amir sits down on a bench from where he can see Shabana's room. The light is still on. Amir wonders if Shabana will look out of her window and see him. After about five minutes, the light is turned off.

Amir pulls his phone from his pocket and types a message:

SHABANA, I AM SORRY IF I SAID SOMETHING THAT HURT YOU TODAY. I REALLY WANT OUR RELATIONSHIP TO WORK. I WANT TO BRING OUR OLD DAYS BACK WHEN YOU AND I WERE HAPPY WITH EACH OTHER. I WILL DO EXACTLY AS YOU TELL ME. I LOVE YOU AND I WILL DO ALL THAT I CAN TO MAKE THIS WORK.

He sends the message from his wet phone and continues to look up at Shabana's window.

After some moments, the light in her room is switched on. Immediately, Amir's heart is filled with the hope that Shabana will respond and maybe invite him back up to her room. But after about a minute, the light is switched off again.

Amir's eyes shift to his phone to see if Shabana has sent him a reply. Even a simple "thanks" or a smiley or "we will talk tomorrow" would mean so much to him. But the screen of his phone remains blank.

Sunrise

Amir stares at the phone for some time and when he is convinced that Shabana will not respond, he starts to cry again. He then gets up and begins walking back to his home.

He walks for a long time and then a rickshaw puller stops near him and asks him if he wants a ride. Amir shakes his head. He does not care when he gets home. As far as he is concerned, the world has already ended.

Amir does not avoid the small puddles on the street that reflect the streetlights, a reflection broken up by the falling raindrops.

He begins to recite a Majaz poem to himself:

sheher ki raat aaur main nashaad-o-nakaara phiroon,
jagmagati jaagti sarkon pe awaara phiron,
gair ki basti hai, kab tak dar-badar maara phiroon?
ai gham-e-dil kya karoon, ai weshat-e-dil kya karoon?

I wander sad and hopeless in this city at night.
I wander aimlessly on the bright lit roads.
How long will I wander hopeless in this city that I cannot call my own?
What should I do, O aching heart? What should I do, O Madness of my soul?

raat hans-hans kar yeh kehti hai ke maikhaane mein chal,

phir kisi shehnaaz-e-lala-rukh ke kashaane mein chal,
yeh nahin mumkin to phir ai dost veeraane mein chal!
ai gham-e-dil kya karoon, ai weshat-e-dil kya karoon?

The night invites me with laughter to a wine-tavern,
Or to visit the bed chamber of the flower faced beauty.
And if this is not possible, then go forever to a wasteland!
What should I do, O aching heart? What should I do, O Madness of my soul?

The turmoil in his heart only increases with each step. He begins talking to himself.

"What more could I have done? I gave her my heart, my soul, everything. And yet it makes no difference to her. What more could I do? I could become her slave if that helped. But I know that it would not."

He sighs. "In the beginning she had respect for me, she treated me well. Because she did not know how much I loved her. Now she knows. She knows that I am her slave. That is why she treats me like this."

Amir stops at a railing at the side of the road and pretends to address a crowd: "Friends, I will now tell you a secret about love. Never express your love to someone who does not love you. She will lose all respect for you and treat you badly. Love is nothing more than psychological mind games of domination. That is it! There is no innocence in love! There are only masters and slaves. There is no fairness. And if there are equals in love, it is for a short time before the master asserts himself over the slave.

'And now, ladies and gentlemen I will tell you the real meaning of 'I will love you forever'. It is the short form of 'Today I *feel* that I will love you forever'. Tomorrow the feeling may be different. 'Forever' may last for just one day, my friends. Or a week. Or a few months."

Amir turns away from the railing and then climbs up and sits on it. He begins crying again.

"Why is there no innocence left in love? Where is my innocent love?" Amir asks himself.

He stops crying and gets up and walks on. The rain falls more heavily.

"Why do I try to draw drops of water from parched wells? You can try all you want, Amir, you will get nothing from it. Your thirst will only increase with your efforts. Parched wells! PARCHED WELLS!"

Amir is completely drenched by the rain but is in no hurry to go home.

"I want to bleed till every drop of blood that loves Shabana flows out. I want to cut out the parts of my heart that love Shabana. I want to remove every cell, every particle of love for her from my being. It is so painful. It hurts so badly. WHY DO I LOVE HER?"

And then he feels the faint vibration of the cell phone in his pocket. His hands rush to pull it out. Maybe it is a message from her! His face lights up.

But when he looks eagerly at the phone he sees that it is only an advertisement. He is devastated. He throws the phone violently onto the road and watches it smash into pieces.

"You give false hope! You cause so much pain to me!" as he speaks, Amir realises what he has done. He picks up the pieces of the phone from a puddle and starts crying again.

"I am so sorry. With this phone I sent so many messages of love to Shabana and I received so many warm messages from her. How could I break it?"

He puts the wet pieces in his pocket.

He reaches his house, opens the door, removes his drenched clothes and lies down on his bed. He stares at the wall next to his bed.

"Where is my love? Will I ever get Shabana back?" he asks himself.

He tries to sleep but cannot. His body is tired but his mind is still feverish with pain and despair. There is not a minute of peace or sleep and he spends the entire night tossing and turning. The hours pass slowly and painfully.

The sun rises. Amir has not slept at all and although he is exhausted, he cannot rest; his thoughts are continually on Shabana and his misery.

He gets up and moves to his desk and idly picks up a book that is lying there. He flicks through it and opens it to a page somewhere close to the middle of the book. He

Sunrise

reads a few lines and a faint smile appears on his face. He looks up, lost in thought, and the smile on his face deepens. He looks down at the book open in his hands and this time he re-reads the lines out loud:

> He who binds to himself a joy,
> Does the winged life destroy.
> He who kisses the joy as it flies,
> Lives in eternity's sunrise.

Peace descends in his heart and his face relaxes. He feels an irresistible urge to listen to a song that he has not heard for many years. He opens his laptop and searches for the song on YouTube and clicks on it. While it is loading, he makes himself a cup of tea.

He sits at his desk and sips his cup of tea as he listens to the song by Rafi:

> *Utna hi upkaar samaj koi jitna saath nibha de*
> *janam maran ka mel ha sapna, yeh sapna bisra de*
> *koi na sang mare....*
> *mann re, tu kahe na dheer dhare?*

Whatever time someone spends with you, consider that their generosity.
The companionship of life and death is an illusion, give it up,
No one will die with you.
O, my mind, why are you not at peace?

Amir's face glows with peace and calm reflection. It is as if a new sunrise has broken the regime of endless night and spread its warm light on a dark, cold and desolate land.

The Future

The time will come when every change shall cease,
This quick revolving wheel shall rest in peace:
No summer then shall glow, nor winter freeze;
Nothing shall be to come, and nothing past,
But an eternal now shall ever last.

From "The Triumph of Eternity" by PETRARCH

The Wall

This story is told in the Ertunty language of the citizens of Yoerzek. Once unheard of, over the last decade, Ertunty is studied by academics and is even understood by some ordinary people, though not by many. As most readers will not be familiar with the language, or even have heard of it, this story has been translated into English.

Note: Something of the culture of Yoerzek is lost in translation. Certain words in Ertunty are representational of what is to be found in Yoerzek, such as president or television, or even the Light Factory, but have no real counterpart in English. Similarly, our emotions such as pride and fear have no corresponding words in Ertunty. However, the people of Yoerzek experience feelings when, for instance, they think an enterprise may fail or when they expect a positive outcome to their efforts. Therefore, for clarity, English equivalents of uniquely Ertuntian words have been used.

Names of individuals and places remain as those of Yoerzek.

4 Tenbary, 3496 pronons after Xectru (21st September 2035 AD)

The entire population of Yoerzek eagerly awaited the launch of Ereino-2. The Great White Wall had never been breached and Ereino-2, if successful, would take Zanikeb into the unknown. This was indeed a great day for the people of Yoerzek and they hailed Zanikeb as their hero.

It was a very proud day for Zanikeb's family and the people of Maderya, his hometown. Whatever the outcome of this enterprise, Zanikeb's name would soon be listed among the bravest of the brave. Many names had appeared before him on that roll of honour; Syangiar, the bravest of all, had even fought the dreaded gondxeos with his bare hands, uncaring whether he lived or died. The brave do not consider the possibilities that exist beyond the act of bravery, they live in the moment where the past meets the future in a tangled web of the indefinite. And never before had there been a mesh as woven with the threads of possibility than the one that now faced Zanikeb. Zanikeb had chosen to be part of this uncertainty. He was indeed the bravest of the brave.

Ereino-2 stood poised on its launch pad, the proud result of pronons of hard work and scientific vision. Waiting to begin its historic flight, at first glance it did

The Wall

not appear very different from Ereino-1; spectators were surprised by the size of its small central chamber, barely large enough for one person. It was the blades attached to the jutting nose cone that made the crowd gasp. Gigantic, they were designed to cut through the hardest substances known to Yoerzek. Now they dazzled the onlookers, the magnificent blades reflecting the brightness of the great Light Factory.

Anatenk, the president of Yoerzek, stood up to make his speech. He spoke of the glory of their scientific achievements and praised the three great minds that had changed the way that the people of Yoerzek viewed their world. Genotoms had lived 300 pronons ago and was considered the father of science. He had discovered a way to measure time and had calculated that Yoerzek was about 40 million pronons old. The origins of their world was still a mystery, but Genotoms had taught them that the inhabitants of Yoerzek had not always existed as they did now; they had evolved from less developed life forms millions of pronons ago. However, even the great Genotoms had his limits and was unable to discover what had existed before Yoerzek came into being. The question of how things were more than 40 million pronons ago remained a great scientific mystery.

165 pronons ago, Atrafun had begun experimenting with rocks that were hurled upwards into their world from the Exalted Chasm. He discovered that they emitted a form of radiation and used this discovery to create light. Responding to his revolutionary invention, the government of Yoerzek built a massive dome that

Shadows of Lost Time

housed the Light Factory that now lit up their dark world. The small eyes of the people of Yoerzek were at first dazzled by their new, bright world but they soon became accustomed to it.

Xertyun, perhaps the greatest of the three, sat next to President Anatenk on the podium and the crowd looked at him in awe as Anatenk spoke of his achievements. He had revolutionized modern science by theorizing that the Great White Wall was not the end and that infinite possibilities existed beyond it.

Although Xertyun had been considered a crackpot at first, over the next 20 pronons his ideas gained credibility and now the idea of life beyond the Great White Wall was a matter of government backed exploration. Xertyun himself had worked on the prototype of Ereino-1 and it had been launched 12 pronons ago. But as its massive metal blades dug into the Great White Wall, they had warped and buckled. Ereino-1 broke up under the force and Xertyun had watched as his dreams were shattered. The mission had failed.

Opinion was divided after that. Many believed that only evil lurked beyond the Wall and that no good would come of venturing there. Others said that the Great White Wall was infinite and could not be crossed. Undaunted, Xertyun set to work on Ereino-2 and there was no one in the crowd more anxious to see the mission succeed than him.

And now it was time. Anatenk rubbed his fins with Zanikeb's and wished him luck on this great adventure. If he succeeded, he would be the first citizen of Yoerzek

The Wall

to venture beyond the Great White Wall. It was a gamble, no one believed that Zanikeb would be able to return, not even Xertyun. But Zanikeb was brave, and would risk his life for the glory of adventure. For Xertyun, Zanikeb was merely the pilot of Ereino-2, his mission to satisfy Xertyun's obsessive curiosity about what lay beyond the Great Wall.

Zanikeb bowed to the hushed crowd and slithered into the small chamber of Ereino-2. He had sat at the controls hundreds of times and was familiar with them. He was unconcerned when the engines began to roar, his mind was already on the Wall. Although the giant blades had cut through substances far harder than the Wall, this was the real thing. Would they be successful this time? Would the blades stay true and strong and slice their way through the Wall?

As the countdown began, the crowd broke into applause. Xertyun sat silent as his mind went back to a similar launch twelve pronons in the past, when the roar of the cheering crowd was silenced by the sickening sound of the blades buckling as they ground into the Great White Wall. It had been over in a matter of tronons and then the eerie silence of failure had descended on him. This day would be different, thought Xertyun, as hope returned. This was a new craft, built on the lessons of failure and perfected by hundreds of experiments over the last twelve pronons.

Oblivious to Xertyun as he sat lost in thought amongst the crowd, Zanikeb waived to the ecstatic onlookers through the small, porthole-like window. Then, as Erieno-2 shot vertically upwards, its massive blades began to rotate.

To Xertyun it seemed that only a few tronons had passed before he heard the muffled roar as the blades began slicing into the Great White Wall. The crowd stared upward and far, far above them they could see, or imagined that they could see, Ereino-2 cutting its way through the solid Wall. And then Xertyun smiled - it was the first time anyone had seen him smile, including Anatenk - because Ereino-2 could no longer be seen although the distant sound of its thundering blades still reached their ears. Ereino-2 had disappeared inside the Great White Wall.

Xertyun gazed for a long time at the hole far above him into which Ereino-2 had vanished. Then he got up slowly and began walking back towards his dome. Zanikeb would beam live pictures back to them from his mission and Xertyun was anxious to view these on his monitor. On his way, he stopped at the Exalted Chasm.

The provider of energy, warmth and light since the beginning of Yoerzek, the Exalted Chasm was the source of survival for its creatures. Though little more than a crack in the ground from which flames and rocks roared upwards, the Exalted Chasm was sacred to the people of Yoerzek as it was the giver of all things.

Though not religious, Xertyun often went to the Exalted Chasm to give thanks, as did the more God fearing citizens of Yoerzek who believed it was the home of their God. Now, Xertyun stood near the Exalted Chasm for a long time, deep in thought. He wondered if one day they

The Wall

would know how their world had come into being 40 million pronons ago. But then he wondered if that question even had a meaning. He then wondered what lay beneath the Exalted Chasm. Was there a way to build a craft that would withstand its molten depths? For Xertyun, the Exalted Chasm was as great a mystery as the Great White Wall.

The people of Yoerzek feared the Great White Wall as much as they revered the Exalted Chasm. For them, the Great White Wall was the door to the abode of the devil. As vast as Yoerzek itself, the Great White Wall was a silent and distant spectator above them all. Every part of Yoerzek lay beneath this vast white dome.

Xertyun sighed and turned away. He must now monitor the progress of his brainchild as it tore its way through the massive Wall. When he reached his dome, he went immediately to the large screen on which the first pictures being beamed from Ereino-2 had already begun to appear.

There was little to see as Ereino-2 cut its way slowly into the Great White Wall. Xertyun looked intently at the massive blades and was relieved to see that they were undamaged. He prayed that they would hold. He got up and moved over to a panel of instruments and as he turned a dial, Zanikeb's voice filled the room. Xertyun had never concerned himself with how others felt. He did not pay attention to what he termed 'petty emotions', and considered them a hindrance to balanced thought and real scientific progress. But today was different. Zanikeb was vital to Xertyun's great scientific adventure and he asked him how he felt. Away from the admiring crowds, a little of Zanikeb's pride and bravery had ebbed away. For the first time, he wondered if he would ever return to Yoerzek. Xertyun cut him short; he did not want any emotions of fear or despair to mar his mission. But he continued to watch the blades anxiously as they cut through layer upon layer of the Great White Wall.

Xertyun sat for a long time in front of his monitor, his eyes fixed intently on the blades and the incredible whiteness around them. He had not slept for several nights now as he had worked day and night preparing for the launch of his invention. The unrelenting whiteness and the spinning blades went on and on and Xertyun's head fell forward as sleep overcame him. But his anxiety for the success of his mission broke into his sleep and a voice in his head kept repeating, "What happened before? What happened before?"

A strange sense that the Great White Wall and the origins of Yoerzek were somehow linked was like a whisper of intuition in his sleep. It was an uneasy feeling and disturbed Xertyun. He woke up with a start and his eyes immediately flew to the screen. He was blinded by the light that came from it and had to shade his eyes and dim the screen. When he was able to look again, he saw that there was a strange yellow glow everywhere. He could hardly contain his excitement. Ereino-2 seemed to have emerged into another world, a world far larger than he could ever have imagined. It lay under a dome of blue and Ereino-2 stood upon whiteness as stark as the Great White Wall.

The Wall

In the small cabin of Ereino-2, Zanikeb panned the camera across the whiteness to something he could see in the distance. He zoomed in and the image on Xertyun's screen showed a board with strange writing on it that he was unable to decipher. The language was English and also Russian. The English text read:

BENEATH THIS ICE LIES A MASSIVE LAKE THAT HAS BEEN THERE FOR MILLIONS OF YEARS. ABOUT 15 MILLION YEARS AGO, THE TOP OF THE LAKE FROZE INTO A 4 KILOMETRE THICK 'WALL', ISOLATING THE LAKE COMPLETELY FROM THE REST OF EARTH.

LIFE FORMS MAY HAVE BEEN TRAPPED UNDER THE ICE AND HAVE EVOLVED IN WAYS UNKNOWN TO MANKIND. IT IS POSSIBLE THAT LIVING BEINGS EXIST SUPPORTED BY HYDROTHERMAL VENTS ON THE LAKE BED THAT PROVIDE HEAT AND WARMTH FROM THE EARTH'S INTERIOR. WHAT LIES BENEATH IS A MYSTERY FOR MODERN SCIENCE.

THIS LAKE IS NAMED LAKE VOSTOK.

The Message

Year 2764, 6ᵗʰ May, 1:35 am

Location: A small hut on the banks of the Urxa Sea on the planet Zespian that revolves around the Chi-2 Sagittarii in the constellation Sagittarius.

The hut is dimly lit, the door shut and bolted. The orange waters of the Urxa Sea are completely calm, as calm as they have been for all of recorded history of the Zespian planet. It is very quiet, as even the water does not make a sound. Inside the hut, two men, one young and the other much older, are talking, almost whispering. The older one stands in front of a large machine that seems to be a computer covered with keys and dials. He presses a few buttons and carefully reads the text that appears on the screen.

"Have you done it, Uncle?" Neb asks.

"Yes, the message is setup and ready to go," Hitu replies.

"What is it?"

The Message

"6EQUJ5," Hitu reads off the screen.

"Perfect. That is what we had decided. Just send it," Neb says.

Although separated in age by many years, Neb and Hitu are drawn together in friendship by two things. Hitu, one of the leaders of the community, is fully proficient in the use of Zigo and Neb was being trained by him and has learned a great deal, although he is not as experienced or as highly skilled as his uncle. While working together they had discovered a mutual interest in mountain climbing and loved to explore the hilly regions of Zespian. Now they are drawn together once more by fate in tragedy.

"Two people with no future trying to change history!" Neb tries to smile.

"But humans must be warned that it was the wrong decision to come here."

"Wrong?" Hitu cries. "Terrible! Tragic! Disastrous!"

In 2304 AD, the human race abandoned Earth to attempt to colonise Zespian. They had had the option to travel to Kentud, a planet in the Draco constellation, and an in-depth study at that time had revealed that both planets have the same atmospheric conditions as Earth and fresh water. However, Zespian certainly seemed more suitable for human habitation as it was much larger than Kentud. In 2304, based on this study, the League of All Humans made their choice. In the beginning, it had seemed better than they had expected and they thought that they had been right to choose Zespian.

"It is hard to imagine now that one of the deciding factors in favour of Zespian was the Singris. Perfect domestic animals they were!" Hitu's face is ashen as he speaks.

Neb begins to shake and a frothy discharge bubbles out of his mouth. Hitu runs to him, holds him, then turns to a shelf, quickly lifts down a box, and opens it. He turns back to Neb and jabs a syringe into his neck.

"I am sorry. I should not have spoken of the Singris, I know that they terrify you." Hitu is relieved as the medication begins working and Neb appears calmer.

"My nightmares are filled with them, screaming, ugly, filthy creatures. My entire family died, squeezed to death and their brains eaten. Domestic animals? No! They are pure evil!" Neb speaks with difficulty, his breathing still uneven.

"They served their purpose for over 300 years. It is our greed that bought this terrible fate on us. The same greed that destroyed Earth has consumed us now," Hitu says quietly.

Singris, although they look nothing like livestock on Earth, were considered to be perfect domestic animals: docile, hardy and, most important, edible. They slither along the ground like reptiles and live in herds, but they are large and strong and can support the weight of the equivalent of four adult men on their backs. They were used for food and as pack animals.

The Singris farmers of Zespian were not content and sought greater profits, as did the industry that had grown up around the Singris. Jointly they sponsored research that eventually led to genetically modified "Super Singris" that breed more quickly, have a greater number of young, are stronger and more powerful. Farmers were able to 'harvest' more meat per animal and these stronger creatures were put to work on building the bridge over the Urxa Sea, a project that had fallen behind schedule.

Unforeseen by the scientists, the genetic modifications had a more sinister effect on the Singris. Along with the positive changes that benefited the Zespian meat industry, they grew more aggressive and became relentless carnivores. Their intelligence increased and, as a result, they became more cunning. In the past, Singris had used their strange proboscis like tongues to suck out the brains of tiny mammals of Zespian. Now, they hunted voraciously on humans to feed their larger appetites. They would destroy whole colonies of Zespians in a single night. Humans tried to resist by shooting them *en masse*, but culling herds of Singris was ineffective as they bred quickly and hundreds would swarm around human settlements, screaming, chirping, pushing.

Even a strongly built house could not withstand them for long. Once they had caught the smell of human brains, they would follow their prey relentlessly, destroying anything that came in their way. With their reptilian bodies and great strength, there was very little that kept them out and they were able to batter down doors and slither down chimneys and through windows.

And they always came in huge numbers, their combined strength stronger than any material produced on Zespian.

Dr Axiino, one of Zespian's greatest scientists, worked hard to find a way of destroying these creatures even as the Singris continued to prey on them and the population dwindled. Finally, a group of 674 men, women and children climbed Mount Cryxten where Dr Axiino worked tirelessly on developing a chemical that would destroy the Singris in large numbers without affecting the human population.

They were safe on Mount Cryxten. It was covered with snow and ice during the Zespian winter and the Singris were unable to climb up to them. They slithered round the base, searching for a way up to the maddening smell of fresh human brains. The ice was an insurmountable barrier and the group of Zespian survivors lived with the shrieks and almost bird like chirping sounds that the Singris made during their vigil at the foot of Mount Cryxten.

After 30 months of winter, the season changed and became warmer and the ice began to thaw. Dr Axiino knew that, with the passing of winter, they would no longer be safe from the Singris. Putting their climbing skills to good use, Neb and Hitu were sent to the dark side of Mount Cryxten that was still in shadow, and where the ice had not as yet begun to melt. Their mission was to look for a ledge or cave large enough for them all to find temporary shelter. Dr Axiino was very close to his discovery and if they could find protection for a few more

The Message

weeks, then they would have a weapon with which to destroy the creatures and be safe once more.

As the ice continued to melt, the Singris slithered up the mount. Like pythons, they embraced their victims and squeezed them to death but, unlike them, they sucked out their brains. Hitu and Neb desperately searched the steep slope for a place to hide their fellow Zespians but on the second night after they had set out on their quest, they heard terrible screams, and the sinister shrieks and chirps of the Singris, and knew that they were too late. The ice had melted before they could accomplish their task. Desperate, they slid and tumbled down the mountain and rowed across the Urxa Sea, making their way to the complex of huts that housed the Zigo machine. Only Dr Axiino, Hitu, the most skilled in its use, and now Neb, who was being trained by Hitu, had permanent access to the Zigo machine. Now that Dr Axiino was dead, it was Hitu's responsibility to recover the machine from where it was hidden, and to use it.

Zespians had failed in their endeavour to save the inhabitants of their world so now Hitu and Neb hope to change history.

"We need to send the message to 2300 AD or before that," Neb reminds Hitu.

"Why not long before that? Why not warn the human race of the disastrous consequences of global warming and pollution so that they can act and save themselves? Why not try to warn them against ever reaching the stage when they are forced to leave Earth," Hitu suggests.

"So what date in time have you chosen?" Neb asks.

"I want to send it to a date before 2000 to give Earthlings time to rectify all the damage that was done to the planet. To go back too far in time would take us to an age where there would be little understanding of the effects of industrialisation and consumerism. Let's randomly pick a date just before the turn of the 21st century," Hitu closes his eyes and places his finger on the screen in front of him, "1977," he reads off the screen where his finger had been.

"NO! That is crazy," Neb cries.

"Why? What difference does it make if it is 1977 or 2007?" Hitu wants to know.

"Because no one will understand your message," Neb replies, "the HV code was not invented until long after that."

"I am hoping that this message will prompt research on the code that will lead to its invention much earlier," Hitu argues.

"It would be wonderful if that happened but there is a great chance that the message may not be deciphered and that events will continue unaltered to the same decision that was made in 2304," Neb is not convinced.

"It will not be lost. If it is not interpreted at that time, it will be stored and scientists will continue to try and decipher it. Mankind may crack the code at any time and then the message *will* be understood. If all else fails, it will definitely be understood by 2304; the HV code was in use long before that date," Hitu explains.

"It is a chance, none the less," Neb insists.

The Message

"I agree, but we have to make the best decision that we can now and do all that we can to try to change the course of history. That is why I am sending two messages, one in HV code and one in English."

"A message in English? I cannot believe you are even thinking of that!"

"Then we can be sure that in 1977, at least one of the messages will be understood, and that the human race will be warned about their terrible future if they do not heed it and take action against their own self created problems," Hitu looks sad as he speaks.

Neb shakes his head doubtfully, "The HV code is a very compact language: your message 6EQUJ5 contains as much information as a 100 page book. The message '6EQUJ5' is perfect: it contains the survival guide to life outside earth and all that we now know must be done to reverse global warming and to make earth habitable again. In terms of numbered intensities, it will transmit all the information that humans need to change their future."

Neb understands that the message will be transmitted at 1420 MHz. Hydrogen is the most common element in the universe and 1420 MHz is the frequency at which it resonates. Long before the invention of HV code, scientists on Earth were aware of this and searched this frequency for interstellar messages, hoping to make contact with extraterrestrial life.

Neb is lost in thought for a moment and then continues his argument, "But a message in English? Are you crazy?! You must realize how much time it will take the

Zigo to send a message that long in English into the past. It will take a year if not longer! We do not have that much time. Those evil creatures will destroy the Zigo long before even a few words of the message are sent."

"I have shortened the text to one page that explains the consequences of warming. And I have begun with an explanation on the crucial algorithm on which 6EQUJ5 is based, and a brief indication of how to break the HV code using quantum computers. We will then have done our best to ensure that humans understand the consequences of warming, and thereby, change the course of history so that they will never have to leave our beloved Earth."

Neb is thoughtful, "It is certainly worth a try, I suppose," he finally agrees. "In fact, anything that increases the chances of altering our fate has to be attempted. How much time do you need to set up the message in English?"

"About three to four hours," Hitu replies. "6EQUJ5 is ready to go; the HV code, as you know, is really fast. English takes much longer to compose and send but I think our chances of success depend on sending them both."

"How much time do you think we have before the Singris find us?" Neb asks.

"I think we are safe from the Singris tonight," Hitu reassures Neb. "In fact, I think it will take them a few days to find us, if not longer. They have to finish sucking out the brains of all their victims on Mount Cryxten and then they have to look for us, the last two humans in the universe. By that time, the messages will have been sent."

Then Hitu adds, "Tonight we will warn the human race that they must never come to Zespian."

15th August 1977

Location: Ohio State University Radio Observatory, also known as Big Ear.

Jerry Ehman walks at a furious pace. He holds a large sheet of paper in his hand. He reaches a door and opens it.

"John, guess what?" Jerry's voice quivers with emotion.

"What?" John looks up as he senses Jerry's excitement.

"Look at this," Jerry hands John the sheet of paper he has been carrying.

John is stunned, "WHAT?! You got a signal?"

"Looks like it?" Jerry grins.

John reads from the paper, "6EQUJ5..."

"What could that mean?" Jerry asks.

"Maybe the aliens are telling us 'you suck'," John grins back at Jerry.

Jerry laughs.

"This came through for 72 seconds?" John asks.

"Exactly 72 seconds," Jerry can't stop smiling, "a perfect 72 second signal, just as we had theorised."

Owing to the rotation of the Earth, the window of observation provided by the telescope lasts exactly 72 seconds, so scientists predicted that any extra terrestrial signal would last for that length of time: 72 seconds.

"This has to be from intelligent life beyond our planet," Jerry adds.

"Or cosmic debris reflecting back television transmissions sent by us," John says.

Jerry shakes his head, "The message has been transmitted at 1420 MHz. It has not been sent by a terrestrial transmitter. I am certain that there is intelligent life out there and they want to communicate with us. This is a 'wow' moment for me." Jerry picks up a pen and circles 6EQUJ5 and then writes WOW beside it.

John laughs, "You received a WOW signal Jerry that will change the world and its future."

"Who knows?" Jerry pauses, "Who knows?"

15th March 2011

Location: A television station, Atlanta, Georgia.

Jerry R. Ehman is being interviewed as part of a series "Aliens, where are they?"

Interviewer: So, Dr Ehman, aliens, where are they?

Dr Ehman: I dunno. Certainly not under my bed [*grins*].

The Message

Interviewer: You have been at the forefront of the SETI program for nearly thirty-five years. Did you ever think that you would find extraterrestrial intelligence? Receiving the WOW signal must have been a very exciting moment for you. I was a little girl in 5th grade and I remember my father being really excited by the newspaper headlines that talked about contact with aliens. My mother was not as enthusiastic though. She seemed to think that the WOW signal was an encoded message from an angel to tell us Earthlings to stop sinning [*laughs*].

Dr Ehman: Well... you can imagine my excitement when I received the message. It matched all the signatures of what we had surmised a message from intelligent life from outer space would have. For instance, it lasted exactly 72 seconds; the amount of time that it takes Big Ear to observe a region in space. It was really a fantastic signal. At the time, I could find no other way to express myself other than WOW!

Interviewer: Wow! [*Laughs*] I mean, that's interesting. Have you ever heard from aliens again?

Dr Ehman: No, we have not. Scientists all around the world have been trying to search for that signal or another signal from that region of space but it has been in vain. The WOW signal never came again.

Interviewer: Why do you think aliens have never tried to contact us again?

Dr Ehman: Why would they want to tell us "you suck" again and again [*laughs*]?

Interviewer [*laughs*]: You must have been very disappointed that WOW never happened again?

Dr Ehman: In the beginning it was great being THE man who received the signal. My friends called me 'the WOW guy'. My popularity went through the roof. Every girl in the university wanted to go on a date with me. But as time went on, and nothing more happened, I began to feel frustrated. I felt incomplete. I needed to know who or what had sent that signal. I have tried for years to decipher its code and, ultimately, I wish to know where it came from.

Interviewer: Are you continuing to search for the signal?

Dr Ehman: No, I am not. I gave up several years ago. I realised that I had spent my entire life constantly searching a small patch of the Chi Sagittarii star group in Sagittarius. That one small corner of the universe and that pattern "6EQUJ5" had consumed my life. The search became too frustrating and I lost heart, I guess. It no longer appealed to me as it did when I was younger.

Interviewer: What are you working on now, Dr Ehman?

The Message

Dr Ehman: Something more down to earth [*smiles*]. I work with an organization whose aim is to educate schoolchildren about global warming and what we can do to save our Earth from its effects.

Interviewer: The man comes from the stars down to Earth [*smiles*].

Dr Ehman: I think this is a very serious topic. I have been searching for life beyond our planet all my life but I am deeply aware of the fact that for all the time we have spent searching, we only know of one planet where life really does exist and thrive. This planet. Our Earth. We must do our best to preserve this home of ours. We must respect it if we want human life to exist and prosper here forever.

Interviewer: Thank you Dr Ehman. It was a pleasure talking to you [*turns towards the camera*]. Viewers, we have been talking to Dr Ehman, the man who received the WOW message from aliens. But even he cannot answer the question, "Aliens, where are they?" Perhaps you can. If you think you know the answer, please log on to our website www.aliens-where-are-they.com. Post your answer and you could win some exciting prizes!

Shadows of Lost Time

Year 2764, 6ᵗʰ May, 2:10 am

Location: The little hut on the banks of Urxa Sea on the planet Zespian which revolves around the Chi-2 Sagittarii in the constellation Sagittarius.

Hitu is working steadily on composing a brief message in English which is to be sent along with the HV code. By his side, Neb attempts to be composed but he is restless.
"I wish we could also send a message back in time to 2500 AD. But not to Earth - to Zespian. At least then we will be sure that the message would be understood. A different message - '78UI6VI' - to warn Zespians against modifying Singris so that we would never face the end of the human race," declares Neb.
"We are on Zespian to survive but life here is not as beautiful as it was on Earth. At one point, Earth supported 7 billion people. But how many people lived on Zespian before Singris started attacking us? 10 million! Earth was our mother."
"My mother used to recite beautiful poems about her beauty." Hitu's eyes are moist as he continues. "There was a poet on Earth named Wordsworth and this is how he praised its beauty:

>'I WANDER'D lonely as a cloud
>That floats on high o'er vales and hills,
>When all at once I saw a crowd,
>A host, of golden daffodils;

The Message

> Beside the lake, beneath the trees,
> Fluttering and dancing in the breeze.

'Have you ever seen or felt anything like this on Zespian, Neb? No. It is a desolate land. We live here not because we want to, but because Earth can no longer sustain life. It has become even hotter than Venus. The greenhouse effect has caused a permanent change in the atmosphere. It was once our beautiful home, abundant with all forms of life, lush fields of flowers, music, poetry," Hitu's voice is full of nostalgia.

"But I agree, it would have been a good back up plan to send a third message back in time to Zespian. As you say, at least we can be certain it would be understood. But we have suffered enough already, why regret something that cannot be?" Hitu is referring to the fact that the Zigo machine has only one transmission module and they were using it to message Earth.

"No. It is not enough to warn ourselves that we should not modify Singris. We must never leave Earth," Hitu's voice is stern, no longer wistful, "That is why we must send a message to Earth to a time before we left it for Zespian."

A long silence follows. Hitu keeps working on the dials and controls of Zigo. Neb is lost in thought.

Finally Neb speaks, "By the time the Singris get here, I will have drowned in the Urxa. They can suck out my brain after I die but not while I live. So many of our people have drowned themselves rather than suffer the slow, terrible death by Singris who eat the brains of their living victims."

"I will drown myself too. But after the message has been sent. I just need a few more hours, son, and then you and I will be reduced to cosmic nothingness. I will die with the satisfaction that I changed the course of history," as he speaks, Hitu's fingers continue to move swiftly over the keys of the Zigo machine.

"If history is changed, then no one will ever know who changed it. Your parents may never meet on Earth or Kentud. Perhaps you will never be born!" Neb laughs. "We may be the ones who change history without ever existing. Our non-existence will be the sign that we changed history for the better!"

"You are getting philosophical, my friend. Existentialist questions no longer matter to me. I must finish this message and send it, then we can discuss our fates and that of the universe!" Hitu smiles briefly at his nephew before he turns back to Zigo and continues to press keys at great speed.

Suddenly, loud twitterings and shrieks shatter the quiet in which they have been working.

"They have come," Neb is terrified. "We cannot escape now. The manner of our deaths is no longer a choice. A terrible fate awaits us."

"The message is not complete. I must hurry and finish it. I cannot let this be the fate of humans. They must protect the Earth and never leave it."

The Message

The terrifying shrieks are all around them and they hear the sinister slithering sound of the creatures as they move in undulating waves around their small hut.

"They have surrounded us. They can smell us. They will be on us at any moment. Send the original message. Press the button," Neb is screaming at his uncle.

"But there is just a bit more to complete in English...," Hitu continues to tap frantically at the keys.

"Press it! PRESS IT NOW!!"

As Hitu hits a red button on the console of Zigo, the door of the hut is smashed inwards and the room is filled with twitters and shrieks.

SETI (Search for Extra-Terrestrial Intelligence) is the collective name for a number of projects whose aim is to search for intelligent life forms beyond Earth. One of the centres of SETI research is the Big Ear telescope at the Ohio State University.

While working on the project on August 15, 1977, Dr Jerry Ehman detected the signal 6EQUJ5 on the radio telescope that bore the hallmark of an intelligent extraterrestrial signal. It lasted for exactly 72 seconds; researchers had anticipated that this would be the length of such a message, a calculation based on the window of observation of Big Ear.

Ehman was so surprised and exhilarated to receive the signal that he wrote the word "WOW" beside

6EQUJ5 on the computer printout. It became known as the WOW signal. No such signal has ever been detected again.

Made in the USA
Lexington, KY
15 November 2011